ALL IS MARY AND BRIGHT

ALSO BY KASEY STOCKTON

Women of Worth Series

Love in the Bargain

Love for the Spinster

Love at the House Party

Love in the Wager

Love in the Ballroom

Ladies of Devon

The Jewels of Halstead Manor

The Lady of Larkspur Vale

Stand-alone Historical Romance

His Amiable Bride

A Forgiving Heart

A Duke for Lady Eve

Contemporary Romance

Snowflake Wishes

His Stand-In Holiday Girlfriend

Snowed In on Main Street

Melodies and Mistletoe

KASEY STOCKTON

GOLDEN OWL PRESS

Happy reading & Merry Christmas.

CHAPTER 1

*M*ary Hatcher had one reason for coming to London. It was *not* to spend a nice holiday with her godmother, though that was an added perk, and it most certainly was *not* to attend the fair on the River Thames. She was there to prepare for the most important day of her life. But her young friend, Lady Anne, had other plans.

"If we wait too long we shall miss our opportunity entirely." Lady Anne clutched Mary's glove-encased hands in the dim entryway of her townhouse, pleading through her tightened grip. "My mother has removed upstairs for her nap, and your mother has hidden in the parlor with her book. We can easily slip out the front door with no one the wiser."

When Lady Anne had proposed an outing, Mary hadn't realized she was dressing for subterfuge.

Mary's gaze flicked to the maid standing by the wall behind them, framed by light streaming through the window in the entryway, her winter cloak fastened and head lowered.

Mary returned Lady Anne's grip with a raised eyebrow. "Your mother expressly forbade you from attending the fair. She fears it will be too rambunctious a crowd—"

"That is folly. Lady Rutledge attended yesterday, and she was perfectly diverted. I heard it from Miss Rutledge herself at dinner last evening. Oh, please do not let me down." Lady Anne pouted. "It will be much more fun with you, Mary. The entire outing is bound to be ruined if I must do it alone."

Mary stifled a gasp. "Surely you do not mean to be so bold."

Lady Anne's eyes acquired a steely glint that was far too mature for the young woman's mere fifteen years. "I mean to see the Thames frozen over, and I will go whether or not you choose to accompany me."

In that case, Mary had little choice. She pulled her bottom lip in between her teeth, eyeing Lady Anne, who stood beside the front door, poised to escape. By the time Mary would be able to make it up three flights of stairs, locate either Lady Sanders or her own mother, and then proceed to inform one of them of Lady Anne's outing, the girl would be halfway across town. Alone.

But...if they went together and made quick work of the outing, surely they could return home within the hour with no one the wiser.

Lady Anne must have sensed Mary relenting, for she grinned widely and tugged Mary's hands. "Shall we be off then? Oh, here, let me straighten your bonnet."

For all her inexperience and youth, Lady Anne was a thoughtful girl.

Mary accepted the help, tightening the strings as Lady Anne inched her front door open and peered outside. Snow gathered down the stone railing on the outside steps and mixed with mud on the street, looking far more unclean than magical. Mary never understood others' fascination with snow. It was cold, wet, and often dirty.

They slipped outside, Lady Anne's maid right behind them, and down to the street where the Sanders carriage waited, its side emblazoned with the yellow and green crest belonging to Lady Anne's brother, the Earl of Sanders. The bitter cold assaulted Mary at once, seeping into the cracks between her seams and prickling her exposed skin.

Once they were settled comfortably inside the carriage, a thick woolen rug pulled over their laps, Lady Anne turned to her friend. "You will not regret this."

It was impossible for the girl to promise such a thing. "You owe me a favor now."

"Anything," Lady Anne said, her golden curls bouncing along with the rocking carriage and her lips spread wide, revealing even, white teeth.

Mary pulled her pelisse tighter around her throat, hoping to stem the tide of anxiety clawing at her. Lady Sanders had done her a grand favor, bringing Mary and her mother to London with their party—and during Christmastide, no less. She was hardly repaying the countess's kindness by escorting her eldest daughter to the Frost Fair. They hit a bump in the road and swayed slightly. It was too late to turn back.

"Oh, isn't it lovely?" Lady Anne's nose pressed against the window, muffling her words. The carriage rolled to a stop, and she hopped down, her grin growing wide, pushing creases into her cheeks.

Mary shared a look of long-suffering with the maid, then followed her friend, stepping over a pile of icy slush to reach the walkway at the park. Though their mothers had known one another their entire lives, Mary and Lady Anne had only become acquainted the week before when they had traveled to London together. Mary had quickly discovered her friend's propensity for chasing entertainment; today shouldn't have surprised her.

Crowds gathered along the rough, iced-over river, mingling in groups and meandering through makeshift tents and stalls selling roasted mutton and hot-brewed cider. A set of steps down the grassy embankment was manned by a rough-looking waterman holding out his hand for a penny.

Mary's stomach constricted. She hadn't realized she would have to pay simply to get in the fair. She calculated what few coins she'd tucked into her limp reticule and how much of it she could feasibly sacrifice.

Roasting meat and charred mutton scented the air, and her stomach replied audibly.

Lady Anne dug in her reticule before dropping coins into the outstretched, dirty hand. "My treat, since you absolutely did not want to accompany me here." She shot Mary a grin and gripped her arm, tugging her down the cold, frozen steps. Accepting the charity rankled, but Mary was in no position to argue.

"What shall we do first?" Lady Anne asked, glancing from one end of the fair to the other.

"Whatever you'd like."

Lady Anne flashed her blue eyes at Mary. "Did you see that woman eating gingerbread? I propose we find the person selling it and make that our first activity." She hummed with excitement, and the crowd—though large enough to warrant the title—was anything but rambunctious, making it difficult to remain overly concerned. Women led their children around the stalls, and men hawked their wares, harmlessly mingling.

One woman, dressed in a blue coat, slipped behind a tent with a young man, her eyes darting behind her as though to ensure she would not get caught.

Perhaps there were *some* things about the fair they ought to avoid. Surely Mary and Lady Anne could obtain gingerbread, look about the stalls selling their wares for a few minutes, and then return home.

Well, to the Earl of Sanders's home, to be precise. He had graciously opened it to Mary and her mother when they traveled to London with Lady Sanders and her two daughters, and then promptly made himself scarce—so much so that Mary had yet to lay eyes on the elusive man. Mother was under the impression that the young, eligible earl was avoiding their company. Since their party was made up of five females, her mother was most likely correct.

Lady Anne slipped her hand around Mary's arm, pulling her closer. "We cannot be faulted for wanting to see this, Mary. An opportunity to step foot on the frozen Thames may never present itself to us again in our lives."

"Even though your mother felt so strongly—"

"My mother will not find out. Cease your worrying."

That was easy for Lady Anne to say. She was not a guest in Lady

Sanders's home. It was far easier to defy one's mother than it was to defy one's godmother.

Resting a hand on her stomach in an attempt to ease the swirling within, Mary sucked in a deep breath and endeavored to release her concerns with it. The joy alighting strangers' faces and the energy among the people seeped into Mary's chest, further lightening the burden of concern and soothing her troubled nerves. Children ran past her carrying a leather ball and giggling. This fair was not only far from raucous, it was harmless.

They passed a printing press boasting leaflets printed on the ice and made their way down a line of booths selling everything from ale and cider to jewelry. But where was the gingerbread?

Andrew Bright, Earl of Sanders, usually excelled at holding his drink, but at present, his friends were testing his limits. Francis left to fetch three more glasses of Old Tom, and Andrew purchased meat pies to balance the strong gin. He slipped between the tents, the hot pies warming his hands, and found Harold waiting for him.

"Francis hasn't returned?" he asked, giving Harold a pie.

"Not yet." A wavy lock of red hair fell over Harold's forehead, but he didn't appear to notice. "I propose a wager. A shilling to the man who empties his glass first," Harold said, taking a large bite from his pastry.

Andrew would fully support a wager any day, but he'd grown weary of the Frost Fair. It was busy, loud, and far too cold. In truth, he'd prefer to sit in his library with a roaring fire and a stack of books, but his mother had made that particular delight completely out of the question.

Andrew dug into his meat pie, letting the warm food settle his stomach as an idea formed, taking shape in his mind. He lifted the pie in salute. "If I win, you can keep your shilling, and we get to leave the fair."

A lovely lady sashayed past them, and Francis approached with three glasses of gin, his gaze following the woman's swishing hem. With his eyes askance, he nearly tripped over a divet in the ice, and Andrew reached out to right him before they lost the drinks.

"Deal," Harold said, taking his glass from Francis. "If Sanders finishes his glass first, we leave the fair. Either of us wins, we get a shilling."

Francis nodded, grinning. "I better win then, eh? I'm not ready to go." Another young woman passed them, and Francis trailed her with his eyes.

Andrew wanted to shake his head, to scoff loud enough to garner Francis's notice. Instead, he lifted his cup. "Ready?"

His friends agreed, and they each knocked back their glasses, chugging down the strong gin.

The smooth liquid warmed his throat, and his eyes watered. Emptying his glass, Andrew wiped his mouth with the back of his wrist and lowered his gaze to Harold's triumphant face.

Drat.

"Shall we have another round?" Francis asked, eyes bright. The man was one drink away from foxed, and the last thing Andrew wished to do right now was drag his reckless, careless friend through crowds of people.

Andrew dug in his pocket for a shilling and tossed it to Harold. "I can promise you another half-hour, but no more than that." He nodded toward the tent bearing alcohol in its many forms. Already his head was growing heavy and the ground seemed uneven. Granted, that could be because it *was*—the ice had not formed in a smooth layer.

"Why are you so dull today?" Francis asked, his fair eyebrows drawn together in genuine confusion. Perhaps the man was more drunk than Andrew thought.

Harold clapped Andrew on the back, pushing him forward. "He's just tired; avoiding his dear mama is difficult work."

"Not my mother," Andrew corrected. "Her guests."

Francis's lip curled in disgust. "She wants you to get hitched, eh?"

"No, nothing like that." Sanders shook his head. "My mother has been respectful of my wishes. But young ladies have a way of falling frequently and needing a lending hand, do they not? Or they often find themselves *accidentally* alone in my library during a dinner party. Or they propose ridiculous parlor games just to get close to me."

Harold laughed with hearty abandon. "Which is why I've found you on my sofa so often this last week."

Andrew's neck warmed. "You can tell me to leave whenever you wish. I hope you know that."

Harold shrugged. "It matters little to me who sleeps on my sofa. The study can be your domain for the rest of the month if you wish. I'd have a bedchamber made up for you if I had one at my disposal."

Francis's mouth hung open. "You slept at Harold's when I have empty bedchambers in my house?"

"It was mere convenience," Andrew said. "I did not plan to stay away so long."

A leather ball rolled between the men, and Francis jumped out of the way, nearly slipping on the ice once again. "Blasted brats," he muttered. He turned to kick the ball back to the group of children running their direction, but his foot slid out from beneath him, and he landed hard on his back, his glass flying from his hand and shattering on the ice.

Harold stifled a laugh, and Francis glared at him before accepting a hand up, eyeing the mess.

Andrew hooked the ball with his toe and nudged it away from Francis. He gave it a few soft kicks toward the children. The boy nearest him paused ten yards away, his cheeks rosy from the cold and a look of determination in his eyes. He lifted his eyebrows in a challenge—something Andrew had difficulty refusing.

Bouncing on his toes, he considered his unsuitable footwear for a moment before nudging the ball into a proper position to kick and pushing his empty glass into Harold's hand. The boy waited, his eyes locked on the ball, and Andrew reared back before kicking it to the child.

The ball reached his target, and the boy grinned, stopping it and resting his foot above it. Andrew noted the moment the game began, and the little boy kicked the ball to Andrew's right as if he was trying to get the ball past the earl.

But Andrew had played the running game in his younger years at Eton, to the detriment of his studies, and knew his way around the leather ball—though his Hessians proved to be inconvenient. He stopped the ball with the tip of his boot just in time, inadvertently kicking it to the side. He jogged after the ball and caught it before it ran into a tent, then he kicked it back to the child.

A crowd of children had now gathered behind the boy, rooting him on, and he kept his gaze fixed on Andrew. He wanted to best the earl, and Andrew was not about to let that happen.

"Don't let him get one in," Francis said behind him, likely still smarting from his fall on the ice.

"A shilling he can get the ball past Sanders," Harold said. Francis quickly took the bet.

The child reared back his leg to the shouts of encouragement behind him and kicked the ball to Andrew's right once again. The ball soared. Andrew ran, hoping to cut it off before it flew into the back of the gaming tent situated nearby.

His foot hit a patch of slippery ice, and he slid, immediately redirecting his attention from the ball to making certain he did not go down as hard as Francis had. He put out his hands to balance when a woman stepped from between the tents, and he ran directly into her.

Andrew's arms went around her waist, grasping her close to him and turning his body as they went down in an effort to take the brunt of the fall. He slammed on the ice, the woman's weight squeezing all breath from his lungs. Gasping for air, Andrew tightened his hold. The ice on his back was a stark contrast to the heat of the cloak-covered woman in his arms, and he was unable to ignore the delicious feel of a warm body against his. He could almost feel her heart beating against his chest—or was that his own pulse hammering in his ears?

"Are you hurt?" she asked, her gentle tone soothing.

He swallowed, apprehension beginning to nip at him. Would she demand recompense for his blunder? Somehow he doubted it. She appeared more concerned with his well-being than her own reputation at present. "No, I don't believe I am."

She paused a beat, and he could hear her slight intake of breath. "Then would you mind releasing me?"

Andrew's cheeks flooded hot, and he lightened his grip on her waist, supporting her as she tried to climb into a standing position. He caught sight of her face as she rose, and his blush only deepened, which was no small feat. Andrew could not recall the last time he'd blushed.

Simply put, the woman was lovely, and he very much desired to learn her name. Her features were dainty, delicate. Her small, upturned nose was faintly freckled, her pale face framed by rich, brown hair.

"Was this what you were after?" she asked, bending to pick up the brown leather ball at her feet.

Andrew rose, brushing dirty snow from his pantaloons, his back stiff. He cleared his throat. "Yes, the children..."

She turned, extending the ball toward him, and he caught sight of dirt along her blue pelisse. He took the ball and dropped it on the ice before kicking it toward the crowd of younglings, heedless of where it ended up.

She brushed dirt from her arm. He reached forward to help her when better sense prevailed, and he let his hand fall by his side. "Are *you* hurt? Can I assist you to a chair?"

Her glittering green eyes darted to his face, and she shook her head. She was amused but reserved—far different from the overly flirtatious women he was used to. "I am well. I suffered nothing but a shock."

"I can well imagine," he muttered, rubbing his jaw. "You must allow me to rectify the situation. Would you care for tea? Coffee? Perhaps a cup of gin?"

Her lips curved into a smile, and his eyes glued to them. "I must return to my friend. I heard the children shouting and wandered back here. She is surely wondering where I've gone to."

"Might I escort you?"

She shook her head. "I think it is best if I return alone." She seemed to hesitate, her soft brown eyebrows pulling together. "Do not concern yourself over my well-being, sir. I suffered no harm, and no one could blame you for slipping on the ice. We are standing on a frozen river, are we not? Each of us is taking a risk."

He commended her ability to put him at ease when she was the injured party. It did nothing but heighten his need to know her name. She was a veritable angel. Any other female of his acquaintance would take full advantage of finding themselves wrapped in his arms.

Perhaps it was their lack of acquaintance—her lack of knowledge of his title and position—which saved him from such a scene. But, no... she did not seem the sort of woman to take advantage of the situation in such a way.

She turned to go, and he was slightly hurt by the ease at which she could depart. Had she no interest in learning who he was? He could see by the fine stitching on her pelisse that she was a lady, and certainly she could detect by his polished—albeit dirty—Hessians and closely fitting coat that he was a gentleman. He was no dandy, but he did take care with his appearance.

"Wait," he said before he could think better of it.

She paused, glancing back at him over her shoulder. "Yes?"

"Might I know your name?"

"I don't think—"

"Please?" he asked, stepping closer and doing his best to charm her with a smile. It had been years since a woman had so interested him. "Just your name."

Lines formed between her eyebrows, and she glanced back toward the bustling crowds eating gingerbread and purchasing trinkets. A sense of urgency seemed to set her shoulders back, and she gripped her pelisse tighter about her neck.

"I will likely never see you again," she said.

"All the more reason to assuage my curiosity," he pitifully argued. He did not request anything from her beyond the possession of her name; it was not his right to even ask for that, but he did anyway.

A grim smile sat on her lips. "I'm not sure this—"

"Mary! Mary, where are you?" a voice called from the crowd.

The woman turned toward the sound as though on impulse, and Andrew grinned.

"Mary?" he asked, and she looked back at once, her lips set in a firm line.

"Good day, *sir*." She enunciated the word to further drive home her opposition to his knowing anything about her, it seemed, and fled with haste.

Andrew stepped back, watching her slip around the tent and out of sight. Mary. She certainly looked as dignified and stable as her name.

Drat his luck. Of course the first woman to grab his attention in years was not only stunning, but he would never see her again.

CHAPTER 2

$\mathcal{M}$ary fingered the pearls around her throat, the hard, smooth beads cool against her skin. After selling every other piece of jewelry she owned, this necklace and a pair of ruby earbobs were all she had at her disposal. The paltry collection was a far cry from the jewels that had adorned her milky white skin just three years before, but there was little she could do about that now.

No, that was not true. There *was* one thing she could do about her family's unwelcome situation, and she had already done it. She had accepted the proposition, signed her name to the agreement, and it was now settled as surely as a wax seal on a missive.

Mary should have gone down to dinner already, but the dilemma of the pearls kept her at the looking glass, admiring the done-over pink silk gown with a gauzy ruched overlay. She really should take the necklace off and save it for a more important event, or she would be wearing pearls nearly every evening that she dined at Sanders House. But they were so lovely, and they complimented this gown perfectly.

Pulling the long white glove further up her elbow, she winced when her fingers grazed the bruise left there by her tumble at the Frost Fair. An image flashed in her mind of the gentleman helping her to stand, his light brown hair flopping over his forehead in disarray.

He had appeared out of nowhere, bowling into Mary and taking her down on the ice with him. Brushing her fingers over her waist where he'd held her so tightly, where he'd protected her from further pain, she could almost feel his touch even now.

It had been clear as soon as she'd noted the crowd of children waiting and the slowly rolling ball that the man had been playing with them and gotten carried away. She could hardly fault anyone for slipping on the ice. But the feel of his arms around her had been anything but frigid and cold. He'd warmed her at once, and she was uncertain if the heat had simply been from another body near hers in the frigid chill, or if it had been due to *him*.

Shame flamed in her belly. She reached up and removed the pearls at once, dropping them into her nearly empty jewelry box on the dressing table and turning away. As bare as her neck looked, it was better to save her one necklace for a special event. Christmas, perhaps? Or Epiphany, if Mama could manage to remain in London that long.

Besides, Mary knew better than to do anything that might draw attention to herself. Father would not like it. She blew out a breath of relief that he was not in London now, that he had not been present at the Frost Fair earlier when Mary had become entangled. Surely she would have received a scolding for it.

She tucked the moment on the ice away in her heart. She would do better to forget it, but the way the stranger had desired to know her name ignited interest in her. It was not his fault he was so handsome. But all the same, it was a blessed relief that she would never see him again.

Her door opened, and Lady Anne poked her head inside the room. "Mary, what is taking you so long? Everyone has assembled."

"I was detained earlier today on an inappropriate errand, and my entire evening has shifted as a result."

Lady Anne grinned, unrepentant. "We shan't give that excuse to our mothers, though, shall we?"

"I don't know." Mary drew up beside her friend and closed her bedroom door behind her. Stringing her arm through the younger

14

woman's, she carefully avoided hitting the bruise above her elbow. "My tongue has been known to slip without proper inducement."

Lady Anne's eyes sparkled, her mouth turning in amusement, but she steadied her voice, sounding grave. "I did promise you a favor. What do you require in exchange for your silence? An ice at Gunter's? Or a trip to Hookham's Library? I know how fond you are of your books and we have a subscription there."

A thud sounded above them, and Mary glanced up the stairs that led to the next floor but saw nothing. "I think I am finished with ice for quite some time." Leaning in, she lowered her voice conspiratorially. "I would happily accept a hot cup of chocolate, though."

Lady Anne freed her arm to walk down the stairs, lifting her hem, and feigning irritation. "That could be arranged, I suppose." They made it to the bottom of the wide staircase where Lady Anne paused, stilling Mary with her hand. "I know how you jest, but you are not in earnest, right? You will not tell our mothers? I want nothing more than to attend the Rutledges' Twelfth Night ball, and Mother has already threatened to refuse me the treat if I step out of line again. Since I am not out yet, she's only allowing me to attend because of her relationship with Lady Rutledge, but if she learns of our adventure today, I *know* she'll keep me from the ball."

"I will not tell a soul." Mary squeezed her friend's hand. "I don't wish to get into trouble, either."

But the deceit clawed at her, and she determined not to let herself be so easily persuaded next time Lady Anne attempted to rope her into doing something they had been asked not to do. She dearly liked the girl, but the debt of gratitude she owed Lady Sanders *should* have trumped all; the countess had made it possible for Mary's mother to feel comfortable leaving her house and traveling to Town, which was no easy feat. Mary might not understand the anxiety which kept Mama home more often than not, but she knew of its very real hold on the woman's peace of mind.

Resolve firmly in place, Mary was determined. She would not disgrace her hostess with a want of decorum. The Frost Fair was not the gathering of undesirables Lady Sanders imagined it to be, but

Mary and Lady Anne had not learned the truth of that until they had arrived at the Thames. They could well have been entirely wrong.

"I have reason to believe that Mother will be quite distracted tonight."

Mary leaned back, narrowing her gaze. "Why?"

"Because my brother will be joining us after dinner, and he will absolutely steal all of the attention. I could introduce a monkey to my mother's drawing room, and she would hardly notice. Not with the golden child present, at least."

"Is he so incredible?" He had made himself scarce for the last few days, it was hard to imagine.

Lady Anne pulled her toward the anteroom where the company grouped before dinner. "You cannot ask that of me, for my opinion is entirely biased. But yes, I quite like him."

"Here they are," Lady Sanders said, a welcoming smile on her aged face, the wrinkles beside her mouth deepening.

Mary stepped into the room on Lady Anne's arm and bid them a good evening. Mother stood on the other side of the small room, a weary look about her eyes. Was something troubling her? As far as Mary was concerned, her mother knew little about their problems— Father had done his best to shield her from the worst of it. Perhaps she was not sleeping very well. They had only been in London for five days, but that was long enough to wear on a woman if she was not resting adequately in her borrowed bed.

Especially a woman like Mama, whose apprehension when leaving her own home for any given amount of time hung like a millstone about her neck. It had been difficult for her to agree to this trip, but Father had demanded it; Lady Sanders's escort had made all the difference.

Mary would have to recommend a nap to her mother the following afternoon when Lady Sanders left them for her regularly scheduled repose.

Lady Sanders rose, threading her arm through Mama's. Their party's lack of gentlemen had many advantages in Mary's opinion, the chief of those being their informal dining procedures.

Mary leaned close to Lady Anne as they followed their mothers into the dining room. "Where is your sister?" The youngest of Lady Sanders's daughters was twelve and had been dining with them while they were in London.

"Upstairs with Miss Bolton. Caroline claims to find our dinners long, so her governess agreed that they could dine privately."

Mary chuckled, taking a seat beside Mama.

The footmen laid the first course, an array of rich soup and braised lamb with sliced vegetables and jellies. Fragrant herbs and spices filled the room, and Mary inhaled the aromas, enjoying the robust meals while she had them. Her household had gradually pared back their dinners to cut costs, and she missed the rich foods and sweet pastries she had once enjoyed regularly.

The women were poised to begin their meal when the door to the dining room opened, and a man came into the room with a pleasant smile about his lips, his pale blue eyes flicking between the women. His light brown hair was swept away from his forehead, the same color as his bronze waistcoat.

Mary managed to stifle her gasp, dropping her gaze to her lap. *Surely* the man who had bowled into her at the Frost Fair earlier could not be here now. Fate would not be so unkind.

"Andrew," Lady Sanders said, a joyous tone to her words. Her chair legs scraped back as she rose, and Lord Sanders crossed the room at once with swift, certain steps—a walk befitting a man who had all the comfort of security and confidence.

She stilled, her spoon poised above her bowl, the soup dripping from it. This man was Lord Sanders? Oh, dear. Hadn't Lady Anne mentioned that he wouldn't be joining them until after dinner?

"Mother." He lifted her knuckles to his lips. "Might I join you?"

Mary arranged her gloves on her lap, smoothing out the length of fabric as her heart thrummed in her chest. Should she signal Lady Anne? When Lord Sanders recognized her, their ruse would be up. He would certainly make mention of their meeting at the Frost Fair, and then Lady Anne's hopes for the Twelfth Night ball would be dashed.

"I did not expect you until later," Lady Sanders said.

"I arrived just before you sat to dine and decided to join you." His voice was harder than the playful tone from earlier at the fair, gathering Mary's curiosity.

She lifted her face toward him, and he caught her gaze, his eyes widening on impact. His mouth fell open before he quickly closed it, glancing between Mary and his sister as if to puzzle out the scenario.

"Did you recall that we have visitors? You have been absent since we arrived in Town, it seems." Lady Sanders gestured to Mama, playfulness shining in her eyes.

"Yes, forgive me." Lord Sanders had a deep voice and a perplexed set to his brow. "I had quite a lot on my schedule. Rest assured, Mother. I do not plan to leave you alone any longer."

That sounded more like a threat than a promise.

Lady Sanders's cheeks pinked, and she smiled in adoration at her son. "How lovely to hear that. Now, I know you have heard about my dear friend, Mrs. Hatcher, but allow me to introduce you." Mama dipped her head, and Lord Sanders bowed before he turned his direct gaze on Mary. "And my goddaughter, Miss Mary Hatcher."

She stilled, meeting his serious gaze, his blue eyes hard. Would he say something now? She refrained from looking to Lady Anne in her fear. The girl was completely unaware of the danger.

"Charmed," Lord Sanders said, though he sounded anything but. What caused him to alter from the amiable man of earlier into this agitated creature?

Mary dropped her head as a bustle of servants brought out another place setting. After much ado about whether or not the earl should be seated at the head of the table quite a distance away from the women, or usurp his mother's place, Lord Sanders sat beside his sister, directly across from Mary. The meal continued, the mothers chatting happily as Lady Anne questioned the earl, and the earl stole glances at a silent Mary.

She could not hold his gaze for long without her neck heating, the memory of being wrapped in his arms just that morning utterly undoing her. But despite her best efforts, Mary could not seem to go longer than five ticks on the clock before her eyes unwittingly sought the earl's striking, pale blue ones. They were the same as Lady Anne's, but that was where the resemblance ended, and Mary found herself wondering why she had never seen a painting of the earl before. She could have been better prepared for this meeting had she known he was the man from the fair.

"We've had to keep the fires raging at all hours, it seems, to combat the horrid chill." Lady Sanders shook her head. "Never in my life have I fought such cold in Town."

"There are some benefits to the weather." Lord Sanders wiped his mouth with his napkin and laid it back on his lap. "The Frost Fair would not have occurred otherwise."

Lady Anne looked to Mary, her eyes rounding and mouth pinching closed. Did she not realize that such a pointed look was bound to give her away before it kept their secret contained?

"Horrid thing, that fair." Lady Sanders wrinkled her nose. "I am certain I heard of all manner of ruffians racing on the ice. One man fell into the river just yesterday if Lady Rutledge is to be believed."

Lord Sanders smiled warmly at his mother. "It is not so bad as that. There are certainly tents which a well-bred young lady ought to avoid, but for the most part, it is just like any fair you could find in Cheshire or Wiltshire."

Lady Sanders clicked her tongue. "Just the same, it is not the place for a proper young lady."

Lord Sanders looked to Mary, a quirk to his brow. "Is that so?"

She wanted to sink lower in her chair. So low, in fact, that she could slip between the floorboards and escape this uncomfortable dinner. Instead, she straightened her back and held his gaze. She was not a simpering, cowering miss, and the earl would learn that soon enough.

Andrew was going to reveal Miss Mary Hatcher—or Mary, in his mind. He could not imagine thinking of her otherwise—for who she truly was. He'd overheard her blackmailing his young, innocent sister and that, from a guest, was not something he would stand for. It was disappointing to have been so utterly misled in her character. Earlier at the fair, he'd imagined her to be a lady of distinction—but what he'd heard in the corridor proved otherwise.

What do you require in exchange for your silence? His sister had sounded grave, worried. Andrew hadn't been able to make out anything else that had been said, but he hadn't needed to. It was enough to know that Mary was holding something over Anne's head, and Andrew would not stand for it.

"I was at the fair today, in fact," the earl said, his eyes holding Mary's striking green ones. They were large and bright against the milky white of her skin, a blush tingeing her flawless cheeks. Panic laced her features, and her gaze flicked to Anne before settling back on Andrew. He wanted to laugh, point, and exclaim that he'd caught her. *Of course* she would worry now that she would be exploited and lose whatever it was she'd blackmailed out of Anne.

Mother's curious voice stole his attention. "I cannot understand why you haunt such cheap, gauche places as that, Andrew."

"It was worth the trip today. I had the fortune to meet—"

"Goodness me!" Mary exclaimed, reaching for her glass and knocking it over. Wine shot from the glass and splashed across the table, dripping down Andrew's cheek and bleeding over his cravat.

He froze, stunned.

"Oh, how clumsy of me!" Mary rose at once, her cheeks scarlet. What was clumsy was how she made her exclamation *before* her hand had even reached the glass. Was her calculation not obvious to anyone else? It was clear as fresh-fallen snow to Andrew.

Mary rounded the table, her napkin in hand. Her eyes spoke of concern, but Andrew saw right through it.

"Finch!" Lady Sanders called.

The butler stepped from the antechamber, took stock of the situation, and spoke to the footman standing beside the door. They moved into action, cleaning up the mess.

Andrew stepped back, leaning against the wall, and Mary paused just before reaching him. He hoped she felt silly. If anything, her diversion had only heightened his need to inform his mother of the situation.

No person would blackmail his little sister and get away with it.

"I have eaten enough. Shall we return to the drawing room?" his mother asked, eyeing him. "I assume you would like to excuse yourself from our company to replace your cravat."

"Give me a minute to change, and I will happily join you."

Mary's intake of breath was audible. Hesitation nipped at him, but he shoved it aside. She'd seemed so utterly guileless earlier that day. But if Mary was innocent, she would not be trying to keep their initial introduction quiet.

"But first," Andrew said, and his mother paused at the door, Mrs. Hatcher beside her. Four sets of eyes blinked at him, and Andrew focused on Mary. "I would like—"

"I am truly so honored to be welcomed in your home, Lord Sanders." Mary stepped closer to him. Her long, dark eyelashes framed such extraordinary, round green eyes it was hard for him to focus. The pink dress she wore flattered her, revealing a creamy neck so bare, he could see her swallow in her agitation. "It is a kindness that I *promise* I shall repay."

The way Mary stressed the words caused him to pause, to search her gaze. She pleaded with him, he could see that. But why? She looked again to his sister, and Andrew closed his mouth. He supposed there would be time to reveal her true character later that evening. For now, he wanted to change into something less...*wet.*

CHAPTER 3

*A*ndrew's cravat took most of the brunt of the spilled wine, and he was able to change it out for a new one—after washing off his face and neck—in less than a quarter of an hour. He left his bedchamber, making his way downstairs in haste. Mary was up to something, and he was determined to figure out precisely what it was.

His mother's cheerful voice sounded from the drawing room, grabbing his attention, and Andrew's mouth fell into a grim line. Mother and Anne were so happy with their company here, it was a shame he would need to expose Mary to them all.

Perhaps he could have saved them the hassle had he only accepted his mother's invitation to spend Christmas at Brightly Court in the countryside. He was certain it was his deferral that had led her to London to spend time with him. Even if she wrapped her trip in the guise of bringing her friend to Town.

"My lord?"

He stilled in the dim corridor, the voice sending pleasant shivers down his spine.

Mary stepped away from the wall, carefully avoiding the beam of light spilling out of the drawing room. Where were the servants, and why hadn't they lit the wall sconces yet? The sun had long since disappeared for the night, and it was darker than typical.

"Yes?" he asked, hesitant.

Mary stepped forward again, her round eyes worried, her expression reaching Andrew's heart. She was either very cunning or shockingly innocent. "I hoped to speak with you somewhere more private. Perhaps we can go—"

A scoff tore from Andrew's throat. Cunning it was. He was disappointed to have been so utterly wrong about her. Surely she was doing her utmost to trap him now that she'd learned who he was. His status, title, and fortune had made him the object of many a woman's aim.

"If you think you can trick me into—"

"*Trick* you?" Mary asked, a disgusted curl to her mouth. "I have no such intentions."

He spread his arms. "Then speak to me now. Here."

"Very well." She spoke without hesitation. "Please do not tell another soul that we met earlier at the fair."

"Not even my mother?"

"Especially not your mother."

Andrew chuckled without mirth, resting his hands on his hips and shaking his head. "You believe you can come into my home, blackmail my sister, and convince me to lie to my own mother? The cheek of it."

Mary likely could not look more appalled if she tried. "What in heaven's name are you talking about? I have never blackmailed a person in my life, let alone Lady Anne."

He quirked an eyebrow, leaning close. "I heard it with my own ears. She paid you for your silence regarding that fair, and I will not stand for it."

She seemed to take a moment to think, her eyes searching the sweeping staircase behind Andrew. He wished she wasn't so lovely. It would be immensely easier to remain angry if her thinking face wasn't so sweet. He could tell the moment she lit upon a thought, for her eyebrows rose, and her eyes widened. "You are speaking of the chocolate, are you not? It was not real blackmail but a simple jest."

Chocolate? All Andrew had heard was his sister asking what sort of inducement would keep the stranger quiet. Surely he had not been so wrong.

"You *are* speaking of the chocolate," Mary said, her voice flat. "I will have you know that it was Lady Anne's idea to sneak to the fair without our mothers' knowledge, and I only went along to make certain she was safe. She is much too young to truly know the dangers in the world."

"And you are old enough to know danger, are you?'

"My age is none of your concern, my lord."

Andrew lowered his voice, acutely aware of Mary's rising irritation, the steady quickening of her breathing. "My sister and her welfare *are* my concern, however."

"Which is why you have been utterly absent since our arrival in London, yes?"

He had to give her a point, there.

"I have never claimed to be perfect." Indeed, he was the first to admit to being vastly flawed. He'd grown up in the shadow of a great man and knew what that entailed.

Andrew was *nothing* like his father. He fell short in every regard.

Mary held his gaze. "We do not need to agree, Lord Sanders. But for Lady Anne's sake and her strong desire to attend a ball, can we not come to an accord on this matter? Her outing at the fair garnered no injury to her body or mind, and she has promised that she will be the model of decorum from now until Twelfth Night."

"Why Twelfth Night?"

A whisper of a smile lit her lips, and Andrew's gaze was riveted by the gentle curve of them. "That is when the ball takes place that she so deeply wishes to attend. I have only known your sister for a week, my lord, but even I can see that she will only be well-behaved as long as she must."

He chuckled. The observation was astute. "You did not know her at all before coming to Town?"

She shook her head. "Our mothers have been friends their whole lives, you know, but this was our first time meeting that either of us can recall. I've heard stories of when your mother visited when I was young, but I can hardly be called upon to recollect that."

"No, of course not." Andrew felt a fool. Trust did not come easily to him, but he could see how very misled he'd been with Mary. Her initial reaction to lying beside him on the ice should have proved her innocence. His neck heated, and he rubbed the back of it to dispel his discomfort. "Are you returning to the drawing room?"

"Yes, the moment I have your assurance that you will keep this to yourself."

"This means a lot to you."

She spoke quietly, resolute. "I am nothing if not a woman of my word."

He could very well believe it. "Then you have mine. I will speak to my sister about minding my mother, of course, but I will not betray your indiscretions from today."

"And you will forgive my...theatrics?"

"Which are?" He knew, of course. But watching Mary squirm was entertaining. He had to assume that spilling her glass of wine to cause a distraction had gone against her nature.

She looked at the floor, her long lashes fanning over porcelain cheeks. When was the last time he had met a lady so seemingly humble about her beauty? He was hard-pressed to recall it.

She glanced back at him, and he stilled, working overtime to swallow against a sandy throat. "I spilled that wine on purpose. I could think of nothing else to stop you."

"You are forgiven."

"If your man cannot remove the stain from your cravat, I will gladly purchase a new one."

"Think nothing of it. I have many."

She glanced at his neck, and he was acutely aware of her piercing look. Had he tied a decent knot? He could hardly recall. But given his haste, he quite doubted it.

"If the stain will not come out, then I *will* replace it."

"Let us save that conversation for another day." His hand came under her elbow, and he turned her toward the drawing room. "I assume our mothers are waiting for us. What excuse did you give them for your disappearance?"

She glanced up quickly. "That I needed to select a new novel. Your mother has allowed me use of your library."

Of course she had. His unaffecting, trusting mother was part of the reason ladies found it so easy to trap Andrew alone in his own house. But this was the first woman to do so successfully and retain both his attention and his interest.

"You've forgotten something," he said, allowing himself to step closer. A warm, floral scent tickled his nose, and he had to force himself not to lean in further and breathe deeply. She would most certainly find that odd.

"Yes?"

"A book."

She chuckled softly, her smile pleasantly curving the edges of her mouth. "You go ahead of me," she said quietly. "I will select a novel and return to the drawing room quickly."

He watched her walk down the corridor in the direction of his library, and he ran a hand through his hair. He was in trouble. This woman was not only beautiful, but she was smart and had an affinity for humor. She was loyal—her dedication to helping Anne proved that—and honest, as far as he could tell. And given the opportunity twice now, she hadn't tried to try to trap him, an *earl*, into marriage.

Andrew's interest was certainly piqued.

He stepped into the drawing room, but his mind remained with the graceful woman in the library. Mrs. Hatcher was speaking to his mother about a dressmaker they had visited the day before, and Andrew slid onto the cushion beside Anne as the women's conversation moved onto the unrelenting fog they'd experienced the previous few days.

"I've never seen so much snow in my entire life," Anne said. "It is absolutely magical, is it not?"

Mother shook her head. "The snow is lovely, but the cold is horrible. If the weather persists, it will be a true miracle if we are able to make it out of London before February."

"We'd better." Mrs. Hatcher's arched eyebrow rose, nearly disappearing under her lace cap. "I will not miss my Mary's wedding for anything in the world. And more importantly, I cannot allow *her* to miss it."

"Unless we move the wedding to London," Mother said, a conspiratorial glint in her eye.

Wedding? Surely Andrew had misheard them. He glanced between the women, but they continued speaking about the difficulties the snow had caused for many of their friends.

Mary came into the room, a book tucked under both of her hands, and she sent Andrew a fleeting smile before claiming the chair beside Mrs. Hatcher.

He wanted to ask her exactly what their mothers meant when they spoke of her wedding. Did they desire her to wed a particular man? Had they schemed to connect Mary to Andrew? That would certainly explain the pleading note his mother had sent to his club, begging for his presence at home one night this week. Or did they have hopes of engaging her to another man while they were in London? Or...no, it could not be. Surely she was not *already* engaged to someone else.

Andrew cleared his throat, and the chatter in the room died down. His mother looked at him expectantly. "And when is this wedding meant to take place?" he asked, hoping he concealed his immense curiosity.

"The end of January, my lord." Mrs. Hatcher's thin face betrayed a pleased smile.

Lady Anne bounced excitedly on her cushion. "Mary is engaged to marry Mr. Lockhart when he returns from India. Is it not so romantic? She has had to wait nearly *two years* for his return." She sighed. "We've done nothing but shop for dresses and shawls and bonnets these last few days for her trousseau. It has been heavenly."

His stomach dropped, and he glanced up, hoping to catch Mary's eye, but she was looking at the book in her lap, already reading the first page as though the conversation around her was nothing out of the ordinary, nothing special.

Of course she had not attempted to trap him. She was already spoken for. He'd finally met the woman of his dreams, and she could never be his.

Mary turned the page of the book of poetry as though she was actually paying attention, but it was difficult to read any of the poems while Lord Sanders watched her so closely. Her eyes skimmed over the words, blurring the letters together until they formed one large, inky mass on the cream paper.

Lady Anne faced her, bubbling over with delight. It was no wonder the girl loved her brother so dearly—he was inordinately protective of her happiness. "Mary, have you settled on the ivory silk or the sage green for your wedding?"

She swallowed. "I have yet to decide. They are both so lovely."

Lady Anne nodded in agreement. "They are...but I do wish you would have added the lace overdress."

Mary wished the same thing. The lace had been exquisite—but even the sale of her beloved emeralds hadn't been able to cover its cost. She had chosen to hold onto the extra money in the case that she and Mama found themselves in need of it. There was a fortnight at least until they planned to leave London—the day after Epiphany—and another few weeks before her wedding was set to take place.

She need only last another month, and then her family would want for nothing.

"That lace was divine," Mama said. "I still do not understand why you chose against it."

Of course she failed to understand. Father had sheltered her from the depths of their financial devastation. Mama might know they needed to economize, but she did not know how desperately each and every ha'penny in their possession mattered.

"It is not too late to return and add it to the order," Lady Anne said, the hope of another trip to the modiste shining in her grin. Their shopping excursion had lasted three days but surely would have gone on much longer had Lady Anne and her purse ruled the day.

"It is done. We won't have time to wait for another item to be made." Mary turned another page, hoping the women would converse about anything other than her trousseau and impending marriage. Her stomach wound up in knots when she thought on it for too long, and she had exceeded her limit for the day. The dresses alone were a purchase she had been loath to make, but Father had been perfectly clear about the necessity of keeping up appearances. She could not marry Mr. Lockhart in a four-year-old gown, and he would expect her to bring a trousseau. But she'd done her best to keep costs down and her new gowns to a minimum, only acquiring the least of what was expected of her.

Mr. Lockhart and his mother were entirely aware of the state of the Hatchers' finances—certainly more so than Mama. They'd agreed to the connection solely for the doors in Society which would open to them; in their minds, appearances mattered a great deal. Father had promised that Mary would do nothing to disappoint, and she had agreed. This was a business arrangement after all.

"Is that what brought you to Town?" Lord Sanders's deep voice penetrated her thoughts, causing every particle of Mary's body to go still. It was bad enough that she'd felt attraction to him earlier at the fair. Now that she learned she was staying in his house, she needed to tamp down the draw she felt to him at once.

"Miss Hatcher?"

She lifted her gaze to meet his curious one across the circle of chairs, the room quiet but for the soft chatter between Mother and Lady Sanders. "Forgive me, my lord. I was distracted."

"It is I who must know better than to bother a person when they are lost in a good book."

She gave him a fleeting smile. "I wish it was the book that took my attention. You asked what brought my mother and me to Town? Indeed, it was for the purpose of building my trousseau."

Lady Anne clutched her brother's arm. "And to spend Christmas with us, of course. Is that not grand? We've only recently met, but I believe Mary to be one of my most precious friends."

"It was just as I expected," Lady Sanders said, turning back to them with smug satisfaction. "When Fanny wrote to me of Mary's engagement and their need to come to London, I absolutely knew I could not let the occasion pass without being part of it. I would be remiss in my duties as godmother otherwise, would I not?"

"Of course not," Mama argued. "But I admit to appreciating your hospitality. It has been far too long since we've been in one another's company in such a way."

To say nothing of the fact that Mary didn't believe her mother would have had the courage to travel so far from home had she not had the escort of a dear, comfortable friend.

"That reminds me of the Christmas we shared when Mary was still just a little girl. Do you recall the crimson *crêpe de Chine*?"

"Oh, yes." Mama's face brightened. "Shall we do something similar for the children again?"

The mothers looked at their children in unison and then shared a smile. Mother clasped her hands together. "It would be a joyous surprise, would it not?"

"I believe so." Lady Sanders got to her feet. "Come, Fanny. Let us leave them to their own company and we can plan."

The mothers huddled together, removing to the other side of the room and bending their heads close.

"I am not certain I appreciate this acquaintance," Lord Sanders said, leaning back comfortably in his seat. "In what other way would we be referred to as children?"

"None," Mary said, chuckling. "Alone, they would not have the gumption, but together they are a force to be wary of."

"Wary, indeed." The earl slid his arm over the back of the sofa behind his sister. "What sort of plan do you think they are hatching, Anne?"

"I haven't the faintest, but I do hope it is exceedingly wicked."

Mary and Lord Sanders shared a smile. Lady Anne's youth was refreshing.

"What sort of holiday traditions do you have in your family?" Mary asked.

Lady Anne sat up. "We play Bullet Pudding, of course. And Steal the White Loaf—though that is not quite as fun without a party, and Andrew is terribly good at catching me. And of course we are used to decorating with evergreen boughs, but I wonder if we'll have to forgo that this year. And then we cannot forget the gingerbread. I believe gingerbread is among my most favorite things."

"We will make certain to accomplish each of those things," Lord Sanders said. "And you, Miss Hatcher? Do you have any traditions in your family?"

"Nothing you have not already mentioned. Well, I suppose..." She paused, looking to where her mother sat at the far end of the room. If she spoke of this, would Lord Sanders think she was asking for such an extravagance? She would do better to keep her mouth closed on the matter.

"Yes?"

"No, it is nothing. I do love the scent of evergreen at Christmas-time, Lady Anne."

"Oh, isn't it the most *lovely* scent of all time?" She turned to her brother again, her blonde curls glowing in the candlelight. "Do say you will find a way to procure some."

"I will do my best."

Lady Anne lowered her voice conspiratorially. "If our mothers are doing something special for us, do you think we should return the gesture?"

Mary looked to Lord Sanders, his brow furrowed in thought. Lady Anne was increasingly thoughtful, and it made up for her impetuous-ness. But who would blame the daughter of an earl for being rash or used to getting her way? She had been pampered for the entirety of her life.

Mary understood this. Until a few years ago when Father's risk lost them everything, she had been spoiled in much the same way.

But circumstances had driven her to understand economizing and restraint.

"What did you have in mind?" Mary asked.

Lady Anne scrunched her nose. "I need to think on it. Perhaps we all ought to consider our options and put our heads together tomorrow."

Mary nodded. "That seems the best course of action." She stood. "Shall we reconvene tomorrow?"

The siblings agreed, and Mary bid them goodnight. She crossed the room to kiss her mother on the cheek, and the older women quieted at her approach. She laughed to herself as she left them. They were quite the scheming pair.

She drew in a fortifying breath as she left the drawing room, grateful the trouble with Lord Sanders was properly dealt with. And though he'd talked of the Christmas season, Mary was persuaded he would continue to make himself scarce after this.

Or perhaps she merely wished for that to be the case. He was far too handsome and engaging, and the way his smile caused her heart to pound was frightening. She was engaged to Mr. Lockhart—she should not be thinking of another man in this way. Even if her short acquaintance with Mr. Lockhart before he left for India had *never* elicited such warm feelings from her.

She made it halfway up the staircase when Lady Anne called to her from below, and she paused to wait for the younger lady to catch up to her.

"You cannot ignite my curiosity and leave me wondering so terribly." Lady Anne grinned, her cheeks glowing. "What is the tradition in your family that you would not tell us?"

"It is not a great secret," Mary said, chuckling. They continued up the stairs, but she hoped Lady Anne wouldn't press the subject. Lord Sanders and his mother were already going out of their way to host Mary and her mother for a few weeks. She did not want to ask anything more of them.

"What is it?" Lady Anne was not going to give up. "Please tell me. I will not be able to rest if you force me to wonder. I have quite the imagination, you know, and the longer you refuse to tell me, the more I am convinced it is something very shocking or foul."

Well, it certainly was not either of those things. Lady Anne had a point—the longer Mary refused to speak, the more Lady Anne's curiosity would grow. Mary swallowed her apprehension. "Oranges. My favorite part about Christmas as a child was having an orange on Christmas Day with my breakfast. I savored it. And my favorite part of St. Stephen's Day was giving the servants each their own orange."

"That is not embarrassing." Lady Anne's nose wrinkled. "Why would you hide it?"

"I didn't want you or your brother to think I was asking for such an extravagance."

Lady Anne laughed. *"Oranges* an extravagance? How silly. Perhaps in Berkshire they are, but not here."

Mary knew the opposite to be true. The orangery at her home provided enough fruit for each member of the household, family and servants alike, and many more besides. The extras were used to decorate during the holiday. But the last few years had seen more hardship, and Father had opted to sell their oranges instead.

She understood the necessity, of course, but missed the citrus dearly. Especially on Christmas Day.

"Goodnight, Mary."

She smiled, watching Lady Anne skip away to her room. Lady Anne had yet to shed the innocence of youth, and Mary hoped that would long remain the case.

Slipping into her bedchamber, she tugged the bell rope and waited for her maid to come and help her undress. Sitting at the dressing table to remove pins from her hair, she paused. A note sat on the table's edge, a breath away from falling to the floor. She unfolded the paper to discover Father's handwriting. It was a letter addressed to Mama, with a postscript for Mary. Her mother must have read it earlier and set it in Mary's room for her to read.

Mary— I am pleased with your willingness to serve your family. Do not forget the promise you made, or what we agreed upon. Yours, Father.

Swallowing, she folded the paper and tucked it away. He needn't fear. She would never forget.

CHAPTER 4

*L*ady Anne squinted at her cards before laying them down and glancing hopefully up at Mary. "Have I won, then?"

"It would appear so." Mary gathered the cards and stacked them in a neat pile. The curtains were drawn against the dark of night, and candlelight bounced from Lady Anne's golden curls, shining on her tasteful sapphire pendant.

Someone walked down the corridor, and Mary looked up at the door. Each set of footsteps that had sounded outside the drawing room door stole her attention, but once again it was only the butler, Finch, who passed by the open doorway.

Lady Anne sighed. "I am finished with cards. Where has Andrew gone? I have not seen him all day, and after last night I was hoping he would be around more."

Mary had guessed this would happen. Men of such distinction could hardly be bothered to remain around a party of women. At least, that would have been the case for her father had he chosen to accompany them to Town.

She did not blame Lord Sanders in this situation, of course, but that did not mean she wasn't disappointed. His conversation would surely have enlivened their evening.

"Can we play the smiling game?" Lady Anne asked, a grin spreading over her face. "I'll fetch Caroline if it is agreeable to you."

"Yes, let's play." Mary continued gathering and stacking the cards while her friend flounced away. They'd played the smiling game, as Lady Anne called it, many times since coming together a week prior. London's cold weather and the recent snowstorms made it difficult to leave the house, and consequently, entertaining Lady Anne had become a chore that fell on Mary's shoulders. Their mothers had become like schoolgirls themselves, stealing away whenever they could for a quiet coze.

Mary hardly minded the chore; Lady Anne was perfectly delightful. And the better Mary came to know her, the easier it would be to hold up her end of the marriage deal. Father's disapproving frown—all full, ruddy cheeks and scowling brow—danced in her mind. The last moment in her house before Lady Sanders's equipage had arrived to convey Mary and her mother to London had been spent in Father's study, and his strict instructions were just as clear now as they were when he was anxiously outlining them then.

Mary *must* obtain an invitation to the Brights' summer house party, or they would lose everything.

They'd had nearly two years to come up with a way to introduce Mr. Lockhart to the elite members of the *ton* as per their marriage agreement. He was possessed of a generally amiable disposition—or that is what she believed from their short acquaintance—and he would be able to make his own way. All Mary needed to do was perform introductions. He'd chosen Mary based on her connections to the Fashionable World and her mother's position as the grand-daughter of an earl. It would take time and care to attain the entry he required, but it was possible.

When Lady Sanders had written to Mama, offering to take them to London with her for Christmas so they might prepare Mary's trousseau, Father hit upon the idea. The Bright family, led by the Earl of Sanders himself, held a summer house party every year stocked with men of distinction, titles, and class. It was perfect.

The Hatchers had received invitations to the house party when

Mary was younger, but since her mother struggled when faced with the prospect of leaving home, they had never attended, and the invitations had eventually ceased.

A slimy dissatisfaction worked its way into Mary's stomach, but she pushed it away. There was nothing inherently wrong with her objective to attain an invitation once again. It was only a party, and Lady Anne was growing fond of Mary. Extending the invitation was bound to be a natural product of their time spent together. Or, so Mary hoped.

Footsteps came down the corridor again, and Mary tapped the stack of the cards against the table. "That was quick. Did Lady Caroline refuse?"

"I am not sure."

Lord Sanders's deep voice startled her. Mary glanced up quickly, and the cards flew out of her hands and scattered, fluttering around her, spinning down onto the card table, and littering the floor.

Smiling ruefully, Lord Sanders crossed the room. "I didn't mean to startle you. You were expecting my sister?"

Mary knelt to gather the cards, and Lord Sanders bent to help her. "Indeed. She went to fetch Lady Caroline for a game."

"And where are our mothers?"

She couldn't help her grin. She tipped her head back to better see Lord Sanders, his light brown hair disheveled but the rest of his appearance spotless. That bit of imperfection—the disarray of his hair —humanized the earl and endeared him to Mary, like he was a young boy with a bit of jelly smeared on his cheek. She itched to correct the stray lock, to smooth it back into place, but shook the odd notion away. "They excused themselves after dinner to plot their mysterious surprise."

Lord Sanders chuckled. "You'd almost believe they were school-girls themselves."

Mary paused. "I had that same thought just a moment ago."

He held her gaze, his hand resting on a card near her. She hadn't realized how close the earl had gotten until that moment, and her breath hitched. The scent of woodsmoke and the outdoors clung to him—not exactly what she would have imagined him to smell like, but she liked it. An easy smile bent his lips, and his gaze dropped to her mouth.

"Caroline has agreed to join—oh! Andrew, I am *so* glad you've come home." Lady Anne barged into the room, her younger sister directly behind her. "You are just in time to play a game with us."

Lord Sanders swept his large hands over the smooth wooden planks, gathering the remaining cards from the floor while Mary sorted the ones she held into a pile and focused on calming her breathing. "What is the game she wishes to play?" he whispered to Mary.

"You'll have to see."

He reached for her hands, stilling them over the cards. "I am not a fan of card games, Mar—excuse me, Miss Hatcher. Shall I escape now before it is too late?"

She froze. A man had never held her hand before, not outside of the brief touches in dancing, and the feeling of Lord Sanders's warm skin on her fingers went straight to her heart. He seemed to sense her discomposure, for he released her and put some distance between them before offering her a hand up. When she stood, she shook her head, hoping to sound completely unaffected. "You needn't escape. Unless, of course, you are afraid of losing."

A sparkle lit his eyes, the color of a cool winter sky. "I needn't fear on that account. I hardly lose."

Lady Anne and Lady Caroline dragged four chairs into a circle. The sisters were nearly identical—the same pale blue eyes, blonde ringlets, and heart-shaped faces—but their personalities could not be more opposite. At fifteen, Lady Anne was a roaring wildfire, while Lady Caroline was a well-managed, contained lamplight. Both of them burned with life, but the twelve-year-old had much more control. Both sisters were beautiful.

"I only agreed to play if Anne promises not to cheat," Lady Caroline said, narrowing her eyes at her sister. "And I will be paying close attention."

"As will we all," Lord Sanders said seriously. "I cannot abide cheating in this house."

Lady Anne scoffed. "As if I would do such a thing."

Lady Caroline shot Mary a telling look, and they both stifled laughter. Lady Anne's record had proved otherwise.

"What is the game?" Lord Sanders asked again, as both of his sisters took seats in the circle of chairs.

"The smiling game," Lady Caroline explained as Mary took her seat.

Lord Sanders groaned as he sat beside her.

"You cannot leave us now," Lady Anne said seriously. "But you needn't be the first to play."

He leaned back in his chair as Lady Anne eyed her sister. "How shall we break into teams?"

"I want to be with Mary," Lady Caroline said.

"Drat," her sister muttered. "No, on second thought, let us play without teams today. We can draw names and leave one person as the winner."

Lord Sanders chuckled. "I will try not to take offense at how strongly you oppose being on my team."

Lady Anne crossed to the writing desk where she ripped a paper into strips and wrote on the pieces. "If you could claim to have won this game at least once, Brother, then I would be happy to have you on my team." She grinned unrepentantly and returned with a small bowl containing folded pieces of paper, which she held out to Lady Caroline. "You can begin."

Lady Caroline reached into the bowl and took a slip of paper, her eyes lighting up as she read it. "Andrew."

He turned to face her better, shaking out his hands. "I won't need to go first, huh?"

She lifted the paper with his name. "The paper decided, not me."

Shaking his head, he chuckled. "The rules?"

"No touching. And whoever smiles first loses. So you must think quickly."

His eyebrows lifted. "That is the only rule?"

Lady Caroline nodded, her young face growing serious. The siblings faced off, staring at one another intently.

Lady Caroline opened her mouth to speak when her brother cut her off.

"What do you think about my new gown?" Lord Sanders asked, his voice as hard and plain as stone even as he spoke of ridiculous things. His fingers brushed along the opposite shoulder, trailing down his coat sleeve. "I rather like the feel of the silk. The pink ruffles at the bottom make my slippers look dashing. It has nice—er...puffy sleeves, and makes me look beautiful, does it not?" He lifted an eyebrow in question and Lady Caroline erupted in a bout of giggles.

"Unfair playing," Lady Anne said, annoyed, while her brother grinned in triumph. "I'll go next." She reached into the bowl and pulled out Mary's name, then faced her friend.

"Remember, no touching," Lord Sanders said, and his sister shot him a glare before turning her attention back on Mary.

Mary steeled herself against her adversary, clenching her teeth and breathing calmly through her nose. She held Lady Anne's eyes, unsure of what to do. If she told a farce like Lord Sanders had, she would likely laugh herself.

But it looked like Lady Anne struggled with knowing what to say, too.

An idea formed in Mary's head, and she rose from her chair, stepping around the back of it as Lady Anne meticulously watched her, straight-faced. Candlelight flickered around them, the roaring fire in the hearth warm behind Mary's back. She brought her hands up slowly, as though she was partnering an invisible man in a country dance. And then she promptly began to dance, focusing hard on Lady Anne as she moved through the motions of a solo dance, her face void of all joy.

Lady Anne's lip twitched as though she fought a smile, but nothing further broke free. Mary made the mistake of glancing at Lord Sanders in the midst of a twirl, and the broad smile on his face made her falter. She tripped over the brick hearth, and a clang of chairs sounded behind her as Lord Sanders jumped to his feet faster than a racehorse and grasped Mary by the arms, pulling her away from the fireplace.

She fell onto his chest, her hand resting just over his heart; she felt the speedy rhythm of his heartbeat matching her own.

"Mary!" Lady Caroline said, jumping to her feet. "You could have fallen into the fire screen!"

"She could have fallen into the *fire*, you dolt." Lady Anne passed her sister to pull Mary from Lord Sanders's arms. She embraced her friend, but Mary looked over Lady Anne's shoulder and tried to read Lord Sanders's expression. Two small lines had formed between his eyebrows, and his eyes glittered, reflecting the flames behind her.

Had warmth flooded his body when he held her, too?

"Are you well?" he asked.

Mary nodded against Lady Anne's shoulder, though she was shaken. "It is getting late, though. Perhaps I ought to go upstairs now."

"I will go with you," Lady Anne said, all solicitation. She pulled away, her worried eyes mirroring her brother's. "Caroline?"

"I'll come along shortly."

Mary bid Lord Sanders and Lady Caroline goodnight and allowed Lady Anne to walk her upstairs to her bedchamber. Her feelings for the family had warmed since their carriage had stopped at her home to pick up Mary and her mother on their way to London. But the way she felt about Lord Sanders far exceeded any sort of familial affection the rest of his family incited in her. Lord Sanders felt . . . *thrilling*, but somehow safe and comfortable at the same time. When he was in the room, she sought his gaze. When he wasn't, she wished him there.

Which was wrong. And must be snuffed out. Mary was engaged to be married. It was done, the papers had been signed, and she could not consider backing out of the arrangement without putting her family's entire estate in great jeopardy.

Lady Anne left her in her room, and she sat on the edge of her bed, rubbing her temples.

She was getting a little ahead of herself, wasn't she? So she enjoyed the feeling of being wrapped in a man's arms, enveloped in his scent, basking in the way he smiled at her—none of that meant the earl wished to *marry* her. She needed to get a hold of her inflated opinion of herself and take the relationship for what it was: Lord Sanders accepted Mary as part of the family. She was his mother's goddaughter, after all. Drawing in a clarifying breath, Mary blew it out through her nose, resolving to leave the young, impressionable, giddy version of herself in her room.

Mary was merely a woman who had not been exposed to many handsome gentlemen in her life. The first young, attractive man to show her the least kindness and she was running ahead of herself, filling her head with grandiose thoughts. Lord Sanders was kind and welcoming. He was not interested in her.

She needed to grow up and cease looking at other men when she was in a binding contract with Mr. Lockhart. She owed both him and herself that much.

CHAPTER 5

*T*he smell of baking gingerbread wafted up from the kitchens and circled the parlor. Andrew stood in the doorway watching Mary and his sisters at work assembling something at the table near the windows. Mother and Mrs. Hatcher sat at the sofa on the far wall, untouched embroidery in each of their laps as they chatted quietly together.

"Andrew!" Caroline squealed, clearly delighted to see him; it did much to raise the tide of guilt in his stomach. He had made himself entirely absent the day before in the hopes that he could rid himself of his slight infatuation with Mary Hatcher. His feelings were not intentional, but he'd hardly thought of anything other than Mary since their first meeting at the Frost Fair. The distance, while keeping him from her actual presence, had done little to remove the woman from his thoughts. When he'd arrived home and joined them for the game in the drawing room, he'd realized at once that it would take more than one day's absence to rid Mary from his thoughts entirely.

But it would be done. It had to be. She was not just promised to another man, she was *engaged*. That was enough to slam the door of possibility in his face as sure as if it were an iron gate, immovable and impenetrable.

"Andrew? Did you not hear me?"

He pushed away from the doorframe and crossed the room. "No, I did not."

Anne delivered a long-suffering sigh. "I asked if you are planning to help us, or if you'd merely like to watch as we do all the work?"

"I would prefer to watch, of course." He shot his sister a wink before he allowed his gaze to trip over to Mary. She focused on the greenery in her hands, but a soft smile tilted her lips.

She had a sense of humor—another mark in her favor.

He scrubbed a hand over his face, pulling out the chair beside Caroline and lowering himself in it. He scanned the contents of the table. Ivy, holly berries, and...was that mistletoe? "What are you creating?"

"Kissing boughs," Anne said with relish. "Mary obtained the supplies for us as a surprise."

Mary reached toward the greenery in front of Anne. "I need more holly."

Anne lifted her eyebrows. "Be careful. You don't want to add too much—"

Mary took an extra handful of holly and weaved it into her ivy. "Or I might call forth an extra prickly man?"

"What is this witchcraft, Miss Hatcher?" Andrew asked, grateful for the excuse to question her directly.

Mary paused, lowering her ivy-laden hands on the table. "You are unfamiliar with kissing boughs?"

"I would not say that." He'd kissed a maiden or two under the spell of Christmastide, but he was not about to admit so here. His sisters hardly need know his past indiscretions, and Mary certainly wouldn't care to hear of them.

She seemed to take his meaning, however. She was anything but naive, and he would do well to remember that. "Then you might know that the ivy, smooth and pure, is a representation of women. The holly, prickly and rough, is a representation of men."

"And the mistletoe?" he asked.

Her cheeks bloomed with color, and she lowered her gaze to the project in her hands.

Caroline laughed. "That's for the kissing, of course!"

"Oh, right." He grinned, satisfied when Mary shared a smile with him. "Now put me to work. How might I help?"

The door opened, and Finch stepped into the parlor, his gloved hands clasped behind his back.

"Yes?" Andrew asked.

"There has been a delivery made, sir, and I wondered if I might have your direction regarding the placement of the evergreen."

"Evergreen?" Anne jumped in her chair, turning to face Mother. "Oh, tell me it is true!"

Mother's widened eyes bespoke her lack of knowledge of the situation. "I'm not sure, darling. This was not my doing."

"It must be—" Anne paused, turning suddenly toward Andrew. "Was it you?"

It was a good thing they were not playing that wretched smiling game, for he certainly would have failed miserably. He grinned, his smile growing wider along with Anne's and Caroline's. His sisters shot to their feet, rounding the table and embracing him fully.

"Oh Andrew, now it will truly feel like Christmas in this dreary house."

Mary looked startled, her gaze dancing around as though she, too, wondered what about the townhouse was so dreary. The weather was miserable, to be sure, but the house was well maintained. It was nothing compared to the wide, open rooms of Chesford Place, or the brilliantly colored walls of Brightly Court. Of all the estates the earl could claim, the London townhouse was by far the least luxurious, but it was still grand in its own way.

His sisters were clearly overindulged.

"The evergreen, my lord?"

"You must know, Finch, that I have no notion of where the evergreen ought to go." Andrew looked to his mother. "Do you have any preference, Mother?"

"None, darling."

"I do," Anne said. "I can direct the servants."

"Might I help, Andrew?" Caroline pleaded, her eyes rounding. "I will be so careful."

His heart warmed. He could deny her nothing—but in truth, Caroline hardly asked anything of him. He was doing a poor job of filling his father's shoes for his sisters. "Of course."

Finch stepped back to allow Anne and Caroline room to pass then bowed himself from the room.

"That was a kind notion to send for evergreen boughs," Mother said from across the room. "Whatever gave you the idea?"

Andrew's gaze flicked to Mary, gratified to find her watching him. "Anne mentioned it the other day. She asked me to do my best to procure some, so I did."

Mother smiled at him before turning her attention back on the embroidery in her lap and saying something quietly to Mrs. Hatcher.

"You have made your sisters very happy," Mary said.

Andrew leaned his elbows on the table, lacing his fingers together. "It was nothing. I merely purchased evergreen boughs and holly sprigs. When we are in the country, we can go outside and cut what we please, and we are used to decorating our houses a great deal. When my sister spoke of her sorrow for missing the beautiful evergreen at Brightly Court, I resolved to rectify that for her. It is the least I could do."

Her brows knit together. "The least you could do? What do you mean by that?"

He meant that he owed his sisters much more than evergreen boughs after his marked absence of late. His father would be ashamed, had he still been around to witness Andrew's negligence. But he did not need to divulge the length of his failings to Mary. "Nothing of import."

She picked up a length of twine from the table and tied the end of her kissing bough, her delicate fingers working to avoid the small berries. "You must have gone to great lengths for the surprise. It was difficult for my servant to locate enough supplies for this pitiful bough. But then again, she is not used to London."

"I may have traveled a good deal to find a proper vendor," he said, a blush warming his neck. "But my sisters' happiness is worth the effort."

"That is admirable. It makes me think I would have enjoyed having a brother like you."

He shook his head. His increasing absence these last few years was a fault for which he had hardly made a dent in the recompense thereof. He could purchase flowers daily for his sisters, and that would be naught but a pittance of what he felt he owed them. "Admirable is an exaggeration, but I will take the compliment."

"But you do not feel it is enough?"

"I am aware of my faults, Miss Hatcher. My family prefers the countryside, and they frequently invite me to join them, but I prefer my isolation. I am often left to my own devices here in Town, and I enjoy it that way." He lowered his voice, afraid his mother would over-hear him. Judging by her chatter, she only had a mind for Mrs. Hatcher, but he could not be too safe. "I cannot remember the last time I spent Christmastide with my mother and sisters. They do not enjoy Town in the wintertime, but they sacrificed their beloved country Christmas in order to spend the holiday season with me, here in London."

"You do not believe they came to help me build my trousseau?" she asked, amusement glimmering in her eyes.

He lowered his voice, leaning further on the table. "I am certain that was a great motivator, but my mother has been trying to convince me to join them for the holiday these last few years. I should not be surprised that she found a way to be with me one way or another."

Reaching across the table, Mary laid her hand on top of Andrew's, sending a shock up his arm and straight to his heart. His chest warmed, his pulse racing, as he lifted his gaze to meet hers. "It is clear that they love you as dearly as you love them."

"But it would be better if I showed it more."

"Be grateful you have love, my lord. Many people go without that most basic, important necessity."

She was being inordinately bold, and it bolstered his courage. He swallowed. "Do you?"

Mary nearly snatched her hand back after Lord Sanders's question, but she had brought this topic upon herself. The rough feel of his hand under her own was warm and comfortable, and she was loath to lose the connection.

But she must. She slid her hand off his, pretending to arrange the leaves of the finished kissing bough to give her fingers something to do. "My Mama loves me a great deal."

The sound of Lady Anne and Lady Caroline chattering happily with the servants drifted up into the parlor, and Lord Sanders looked toward the door.

She relaxed a fraction, believing it to the end of the topic.

"That is all?" he pressed, to her surprise. "I seem to recall hearing about an engagement."

"Which is none of your concern, my lord."

He chuckled, leaning back. "You'll forgive me. I have a very curious nature."

"That is not a fault, exactly. As long as you curb your desire to yield to that curious nature."

"And how do you suggest I do that?"

She raised an eyebrow. "Perhaps you might start with refraining from asking impertinent questions."

"I shall," he agreed, dipping his head, but his eyes locked on hers. She wondered if he meant it. "Will you forgive me?"

"Of course."

Lord Sanders's mouth quirked into a smile. "Friends?"

Were they? Mary would like to be, of course. And she imagined now that their mothers had been happily reunited, their families were bound to see more of one another in the future. Indeed, she needed that to be the case if she was to accomplish the task which Father had given her. But looking into Lord Sanders's guileless countenance made her agreement with Father seem dishonorable. She shook the thought. What did it matter? She hardly had a choice now but to follow through.

And if she could become friends with Lord Sanders, securing a coveted invitation to his summer house party next year, for Mary *and* her betrothed, would be infinitely easier.

"Yes," she agreed. "Friends."

Lady Caroline barreled into the room, a length of evergreen in her arms. "I want to put this on the mantel, Andrew. Will you help me?"

He rose at once and moved to aid his sister. Mary took advantage of his distraction to slip from the room, carrying the mistletoe with her. She found that the greater the distance she put between herself and Lord Sanders, the more easily she could breathe. He was kind, thoughtful, handsome, and intelligent. And she needed to remember that he would forever remain her friend—but nothing more.

Lady Anne's voice carried, making her easy to locate, and within a few minutes, they were discussing the best location for the kissing bough.

"I think the archway that leads into the drawing room would be splendid." Lady Anne wrinkled her nose in thought. "Or perhaps along the ceiling at the base of the stairs?"

"Either place would look lovely, of course," Mary said.

Lady Anne grinned impishly. "The base of the stairs, then. I'm more likely to catch one of Andrew's friends that way if they ever come visiting."

Mary laughed, hoping the servants hadn't overheard. "You don't want to be caught kissing a man before you are fully out in society, Lady Anne. Or even *after* you are out. You have your reputation to consider."

"Don't say such things," the girl said with a pout. "You sound very much like Miss Bolton when you do."

Mary didn't appreciate being compared to the Bright girls' governess, but she owned that it was rightfully earned. She could only hope Lady Anne understood the importance of protecting her reputation, that she did not feel it was a duty which could easily be dismissed.

Without a good reputation, what did a woman have?

"We need Andrew's help. One moment. I shall fetch him."

Mary held the kissing bough to her chest, descending the stairs to await her friend. Or was it *friends* now?

Lady Anne returned shortly with Lord Sanders and Lady Caroline; the gentleman watched her so closely, she longed for a looking glass. Had she something in her teeth? Or a spot on her cheek?

"Where am I hanging this lovely creation?" he asked, reaching for the bough in her hands.

"Just there." Lady Anne pointed to the exact place she wanted it to hang, and her brother craned his neck to see.

Reaching up, he was a few feet shy of the necessary height. "I'll need a chair."

"I'll fetch one!" Lady Caroline ran from the room, returning shortly with a ladder-back chair precariously wobbling in her arms. She placed it at the base of the stairs with a thud.

Lord Sanders stepped onto the chair and reached up, his height an added benefit in this scenario. He paused and glanced down at the women. "How are men supposed to take a berry when the mistletoe is out of their reach?"

"Oh, drat." Lady Anne's forehead scrunched in thought. She brightened. "The doorway to the drawing room, then?"

"The doorway is a perfect location, and entirely reachable."

No one seemed to find fault with the idea that men would actually be plucking berries from the bough. Who did Lord Sanders expect to come kissing his sisters? Or who did *he* expect to kiss?

Lady Caroline removed the chair, and the women followed Lord Sanders upstairs to the drawing room, watching as he hung the kissing bough on the wall above the doorway.

"It is so lovely," Lady Caroline said softly.

"I do hope we have gentlemen callers soon," Lady Anne added, a wistfulness to her voice.

Lord Sanders looked to his sister with startled disgust, and Mary quickly strung her arm through Lady Anne's. So perhaps he was jesting about the berries after all. "But we shan't kiss any of them, shall we?"

Lady Anne's lips fell into a flat line, and she shook her head. Mary shared a look with Lord Sanders and imagined he felt the same way she did: there would be no stopping Lady Anne. Perhaps they ought to refrain from having any men visit in the next fortnight until Twelfth Night had passed and the mistletoe was removed.

"Shall we play the smiling game now?" Lady Caroline asked, bouncing on her toes.

"I have a better idea," Lord Sanders said. "I thought we could introduce Miss Hatcher to a Bright family tradition."

The way he looked at Mary caused a volley of shivers to move down her back. His blue eyes were dancing, amused, and steadily trained on her. She needed to be careful, or she was bound to find herself utterly lost in their depths.

Lady Anne tilted her head to the side. "Which one?"

"The stocking carolers."

Lady Caroline and Lady Anne squealed in unison, but Mary only felt more ignorant.

"Shall I fetch the paper for the hats?" Lady Anne asked, clapping her hands together. "I saw some in the library just yesterday."

Lady Caroline turned for the stairs. "And I will gather the stockings."

"Not yet," Lord Sanders said. "We must practice first without them."

"Will no one explain this to me?" Mary asked, careful to contain her laughter. The siblings were quite the force when their heads bent together, and it both heartened Mary and caused her envy. Perhaps one day when she had children of her own, she could foster the sort of relationship between them that she witnessed in Lord Sanders's household.

"It will be great fun," Lady Caroline said, lifting Mary's hand in hers. "We are putting on a Christmas puppet show!"

CHAPTER 6

*C*hristmas dawned overcast and white. Large, fluffy flakes fell lazily to the ground outside, coating railings and rooftops with pure white snow. Andrew pulled the drapes open more fully over the dining room window and swept his gaze along the flawlessly white-capped building across from their townhouse. He'd been up before the sun, and he could hardly wait for the women to rise and come down to breakfast.

When Mary had failed to share her favorite tradition with them, Andrew had wanted to pry, to learn what she was not telling him, but his sense as a gentleman forbade him from doing so. It had been luck alone that he'd left the drawing room in time to hear Anne asking that very question on the staircase.

His sister's ignorance aside, he could well understand why Mary didn't want her hosts to think she was asking for any sort of extravagance. She was humble, and that sort of humility gave Andrew the strongest urge to do something kind for her.

Turning to lean against the window sill, Andrew crossed his arms over his chest. The oranges sitting in the center of each plate at the table were bright against the dark evergreen boughs making up the centerpiece, red holly berries strewn throughout.

Footsteps coming down the corridor warned him of someone's impending arrival and Andrew stood, straightening with anticipation. Mary stepped into the room and stopped short, her gaze riveted on the table. Her eyes were as wide and round as the oranges she stared at.

Andrew cleared his throat, and she glanced up sharply, her cheeks rounding as she smiled.

"Good morning, Miss Hatcher."

She dipped in a curtsy. "Good morning, my lord. And what a lovely day it is looking to be."

Lifting a hand to halt the footman standing against the far wall, Andrew stepped forward to pull out a chair for Mary.

She paused, resting her hand on the table's edge and peering up at him. "Did you know?"

He froze, caught. She was referring to the oranges. She must be. Rubbing the back of his neck, he glanced down. "I did."

"From your sister?"

"No." This continued to worsen. What kind of man would she believe him to be? He could lie...but, no. If nothing else, he *was* honest. "I overheard your conversation with Anne on the stairs that evening."

Her lips bent into a grim line. "I did not intend to influence your plans—"

Andrew cupped her shoulder. "Please. You are our guest. It was the least I could do, and I am certain my sisters will adore the treat as well."

Her gaze lowered. "Then I must thank you. It has been a few years since I've enjoyed an orange on Christmas morning." She lifted the orange from her plate, turning it around in her hands. "You cannot know how much I've missed it."

Andrew cleared his throat, hoping to dispel the thick air between them. Why had it been years? Had she not mentioned oranges to be her favorite part of Christmas morning? And the subsequent offering of the fruit to her servants on St. Stephen's Day? These were questions he did not have a right to ask.

Mary moved out of his reach, his hand slipping free of her shoulder, and took her seat. He stepped around the table and sat across from her, putting some distance between them.

"Miss Hatcher, you will forgive my impertinence—"

"Oranges!" Caroline said, sweeping into the room, Anne behind her.

Anne glanced from the fruit to Mary, taking a seat beside her friend. "Mary, it is just as you wished!"

Mary glanced to Andrew and then back to her plate, a soft smile on her lips. "I feel very fortunate, Lady Anne."

Clicking heels carried their mothers into the room a moment later, and the party was settled. Andrew tried to keep his gaze on his own plate, but he could not help watching Mary carefully peel her orange and divide it into segments, the acidic scent filling the room. The way she managed the job with tender care was mesmerizing, and Andrew would have liked to sit and watch her all day.

"We have a surprise for you, Mama," Caroline said.

"Later this afternoon. After your nap, perhaps?" Anne added.

Andrew gestured to their guests. "It is a surprise for both of the mothers."

Mother leaned closer to Mrs. Hatcher. "These children are so sweet. We have been utterly remiss in keeping them apart the last twenty years."

"I would have to agree," Mrs. Hatcher said, guilt falling over her face. "And I am sorry for it."

Mother's sad smile reached her eyes, and she took her friend's hand. They shared a silent moment before turning their attention toward the oranges on their plates. Andrew caught Mary's eye over the table, noting the faint lines forming between her soft brown eyebrows. What could Mrs. Hatcher have meant by assuming responsibility for their separation? Surely she had not *intentionally* kept the families apart.

Anne stole his attention, and he dragged his gaze from Mary. She whispered so the mothers wouldn't hear her. "We must prepare. We haven't practiced the songs yet."

"We can practice while we fold the hats." Andrew peeled his

orange, the tangy citrus further scenting the air as each of the women did the same thing. There were dishes of ham, coddled eggs, and toasted bread waiting to be served, but the occupants of the room were focused on their fruit.

He had a feeling this was going to become a tradition in the Bright household as well. And he was absolutely determined to discover why it had ceased for the Hatchers.

"I cannot fold a hat to save my life." Mary dropped the creased paper on the card table and leaned back in her seat, shaking her head at Lady Anne. The newsprint was meant to be a miniature hat, but instead, it was a crumpled sheet of limp paper with too many crease lines and no discernable shape.

Lady Anne flashed her bright white teeth as the afternoon sun streamed through the window and lit her face. "Shall I show you again?"

"You may, but it would be for naught. Folding paper hats is not one of my talents."

"What is one of your talents, then?" Lord Sanders asked. He leaned over in his seat near the fire, making it easier for Mary to see him around Lady Anne's chair.

Mary lifted the crumpled sheet of newsprint again and pretended to analyze it. "You cannot expect me to answer that ridiculous question."

Lady Anne scoffed. "What is so ridiculous about recognizing your own talents?"

"It is not in the least humble."

"There, we've found talent number one: humility." Lord Sanders rose from his seat and took the chair beside Mary, watching her with a scrutiny that sent prickles down her back.

"I am not hum—"

"No arguing," Lord Sanders admonished. "If you will not own your talents, we shall have to figure them out for ourselves."

Lady Anne laughed. "Are we to guess, then? Just from the sound of your voice, I'm certain you can sing quite well."

"No, no guessing," Lord Sanders said, lifting a hand to stop his sister. "Not unless they are educated guesses, Anne. Otherwise, we could list every general accomplishment until we discover the correct ones, and that is far too easy."

She pouted. "I am certain I'm correct about the singing, at least."

She wasn't, though. Mary tried to keep her mirth from showing on her face, but she knew she could not sing well. And the way Lady Anne regarded her now with narrowed eyes and drawn brows was evidence that she wouldn't believe Mary anyway if she *did* admit that truth aloud. Lady Anne would probably force Mary to sing to prove her claim.

Lady Anne tilted her head. "Are you adept with a needle?"

"Anne," Lord Sanders said, drawing out the word as he dipped his chin. "That is cheating."

She grunted, then snatched the paper from Mary's grip and proceeded to fold it into something that resembled a miniature hat.

Lady Caroline entered the room, a sheet of paper in her hands. "I've written out the words to the songs for Mary. Are you finished with the puppets yet?"

Lady Anne brightened. She shot her brother a smug grin. "I suppose we'll find out soon enough if Mary sings like a nightingale or screeches like a pig, shan't we?"

She was bound to be disappointed when Mary finally sang for her. Mary's voice, while not akin to the screeching of a pig, did not sound smooth or velvety. It was basic. It was bland. It was *not* a talent.

"We are not finished with the puppets," Lord Sanders said, ignoring Lady Anne. "Have you brought the buttons, Caro?"

Her little nose scrunching up, Lady Caroline dropped her papers on the table. "I forgot the buttons. Give me a few minutes. I'm certain I can find some quickly."

"It is rather limp, but it's better than nothing." Lady Anne gave Mary the folded miniature hat that would adorn her stocking puppet; Mary had to bite back a smile at the sad creation. It would likely look much better if Mary hadn't folded it to death before Lady Anne could get around to fixing it.

"We ought to keep these puppets in case we return to London for Christmas next year." Lady Anne reached for a stocking on the table and turned it over in her hands. "It is really too bad I didn't think to bring our old puppets."

Mary shifted in her seat, turning the small hat around in her fingers. She was not blessed with siblings, and the camaraderie between the Bright children was endearing. Lord Sanders clearly loved his sisters, and they looked up to him. But there was something else there, too, something that made Mary wish to be welcomed into their inner circle. There was a sense of belonging and comfort between the three. That they knew so well they were loved and accepted, that they could be or say whatever they wished, was something she envied.

Mary hadn't felt that sort of unequivocal approval in her entire life.

Lady Caroline bounced into the room. "Buttons!"

"Did you bring sewing supplies?"

Lady Caroline halted mid-step and stared at her sister.

Lady Anne sighed. "I'll fetch my sewing basket." She slipped from the room, and Lady Caroline took her seat, dropping her buttons on the tabletop and organizing them into sets of two.

"They won't all match, but they will be close enough."

"That will make the puppets even sweeter," Mary said, leaning forward to look at the array of round, colored buttons.

Lord Sanders lifted a stocking and dropped it over his sister's forehead, eliciting giggles from the girl. "We must move quickly if we are going to have enough time to assemble the baskets for St. Stephen's Day."

Mary paused, her fingertips digging into the edges of a navy-blue, wooden button. She'd loved distributing treats and gifts to the servants on St. Stephen's Day more than receiving her own from her parents in years past, but the last few Christmases, the economies her family had been forced to exercise had left the servants with very little.

It had been shameful delivering gifts the last few years that hardly warranted the name. She relaxed her grip on the button, the prospect of assembling decent baskets filling her with anticipation. "Then let us practice the song."

"Agreed," Lord Sanders said, shooting Mary a mischievous smile.

She dipped her head and took a sheet of paper from Lady Caroline, running her gaze over the lyrics written out in a neat, even script. They weren't a creation of the Bright children as she'd imagined, but well-known Christmas carols.

Mary lowered the sheet of paper. "I know these songs."

"Very good," Lord Sanders said. "Then we will only need to practice once."

"What are the puppets to do?" she asked.

Lady Caroline slipped a stocking over her hand. "They are the carolers."

"And the purpose of the hats?" Mary asked, lifting a small, folded hat.

"To make them look adorable, of course."

Lady Anne glided back into the room and took the last available seat at the card table, plopping her sewing basket in the center of it. She shot Mary a mockingly stern glance. "Carolers mustn't go caroling without proper hats, Mary. It isn't done."

A grin spread over Mary's lips, her chest warming. She accepted a needle and thread from Lady Anne and began sewing button eyes onto her stocking caroler. Her mother had great difficulty leaving the comfort of her house for anything other than church and was shy around others—save Lady Sanders, clearly—so Mary's opportunities to spend time with other families had long been limited to those within their parish whom they would invite to dine. They boasted acquaintanceship with an earl and a baron in the immediate vicinity, and a slew of gentility, which gave Mary all the socialization she'd ever felt she had needed. But now, witnessing the camaraderie and love between the Bright siblings, Mary longed for close relationships such as these.

In the short time they'd spent together, Lady Anne and Lady Caroline had grown to feel more like sisters than friends.

Lady Anne settled into her seat with her needle and thread, a playful tilt to her lips. Golden ringlets brushed her temples, bouncing along with her enthusiasm. "Mary, you hardly speak about your betrothed, and I'm rather dying to know more about him."

Mary swallowed, a measure of the warmth she'd noted only moments before suddenly dissipating. What an abrupt change of topic, and not one she could easily speak on. She hardly knew Mr. Lockhart herself. There wasn't much she would be able to share. She could describe her soon-to-be mother-in-law, but she had a feeling the Bright siblings would not be interested in that knowledge.

Pinching the cool needle between her fingers, Mary focused on stringing the thread through the eye. "What would you like to know?"

Lady Anne looked aghast that Mary even needed to ask. "Well, everything, of course!"

CHAPTER 7

*A*ndrew perked up, keeping his focus on the buttons in his hand. Curiosity swirled in his stomach, pressing up against his chest; it took a great deal of effort not to press Mary for more information himself. But he shamefully wished to know more about the man Mary Hatcher had agreed to marry. Andrew assumed this Mr. Lockhart was exemplary in every form—for only a perfect man would deserve someone as wonderful as Mary. *She* was amazing in every regard.

Humble. Kind. Caring. Beautiful.

Did Mary have any faults?

"I'm not sure what to say," she said, her focus preoccupied with the needle she was threading.

Anne bounced in her seat. "What does he look like?"

"Well...he has dark hair—so dark it appears black. His nose is straight, and his eyes are dark brown."

"But is he handsome?"

"Oh, yes." Mary nodded. "At least, I haven't seen Mr. Lockhart in nearly two years, but he was quite handsome when last we met."

Andrew stiffened. Mary had not seen the man in two years? What could divide her from her betrothed for such a length of time? There was no way she had contracted a marriage of convenience. It couldn't be.

Andrew's gaze flicked to Mary's, but her eyes were downcast, her cheeks glowing pink. He wanted to question her further, but her discomfort was evident. It was yet another sign of her refreshing humility—a trait so seldom seen in London's drawing rooms.

A prickle of unease ran through his core and tightened like a snake around its prey. His gaze trailed the gentle slope of her nose, the dust of a blush on her cheekbones, as the truth settled on him: he had found her too late.

Why was fate so cruel as to show Andrew the perfect woman after she had made a commitment to another man?

"Is he amusing?" Anne asked.

Mary tilted her head in thought. "I am not entirely sure, actually."

"Andrew tends to be *very* silly," Caroline said to Mary, her tone brooking no argument. "Especially when he is meant to be serious. So be mindful of your puppet during the performance and secure a position far from his if you can help it."

"It has been a few years since we've done one of these puppet shows." Andrew tried to sound hurt, and he laid his palm over his heart. "You cannot believe me to be so silly *now*."

Caroline looked disbelieving, and Anne ignored him. But Mary gave him a small, amused smile.

If only he'd met her before. But now what could he do? He held her smile, the answer swimming before him as clear as Mary's green eyes. There was nothing left but to be her friend.

Finch opened the door, stepping inside the room and silently waiting for acknowledgment.

"What is it?" Andrew asked, causing his sisters to follow his gaze toward their waiting butler.

"You have visitors, my lord."

Andrew lifted an eyebrow. He hadn't had any visitors at the townhouse in quite some time—not since before his mother and sisters had arrived. "Are they here for my mother?"

"You have been specifically requested, my lord."

"Did they bring a card?"

Finch shook his head. "A Mr. Harold Pinnegar and a Mr. Francis Jacobs, my lord."

"Ah, of course. Tell them I'll be right down."

Finch nodded before retreating to the tune of Caroline's disappointment. "But we have yet to practice, Andrew."

"I'll see what they need and send them on their way. It should only be a moment."

Anne sat up in her seat. "Should we not invite them to stay for a visit?"

Andrew paused, sweeping his gaze over his sister. At fifteen she was already too eager to form a connection, and it was dangerous. She was too beautiful to be ignored by London men and too naive to understand them.

She was trouble now, and she was likely going to become more so by the time she came of age. "If you are hoping to sneak in a meeting with one of them under the kissing bough, you are bound to become disappointed, Anne."

She scrunched her nose, and Mary chuckled beside her. Andrew shot Mary a knowing grin before quitting the room, the sound of feminine laughter trailing behind his hurried steps. He hadn't seen his friends since the day of the Frost Fair, and he was fairly certain they'd only sought him out now because they were bored and knew his cook made an incredible roast duck.

Finch stood in the corridor, directing Andrew to where his friends awaited him in the library. He found them settled comfortably, Francis leaning an elbow on the fireplace mantel and Harold reclining in a leather wingback chair, his legs stretched forward and crossed at the ankles.

"Good afternoon, gentlemen."

They both dipped their heads in acknowledgment. "My sofa has been empty these last few nights," Harold said. "Needed to make sure your mother wasn't holding you here against your will."

"How generous of you." Andrew stepped around Harold's feet and dropped into the chair beside his. "But no one has that sort of authority over me."

"Not even your mama?" Francis asked, crossing his arms over his chest and moving toward the settee on the other side of the rug. "Was it not her letter that forced you home just a few days ago?"

"I am spending Christmas with my family."

Harold and Francis shared a look.

"What is it?" Andrew asked, glancing between his friends. "There is nothing wrong with that."

"No, of course not," Harold agreed.

Francis rubbed his chin. "And when was the last time you spent any length of time with your mother?"

His jaw clenched, his gut reminding him that his friends were only being playful—that they did not know the depth of his guilt. But still, he could not refrain from arguing his case. "I go to Brightly Court every summer for her house party."

Francis lifted his hands in surrender. "Just doing my best to vex you, my good man. No need to get your hackles up."

Andrew leaned back against the cushion, hoping to appear at ease, the scent of the evergreen needles on the mantel wafting to his nose. "What do you men have planned this evening?"

"That depends entirely upon you, my friend," Francis said, grinning. "We've heard tell of a little place in Cheapside that just opened. A faro club. Interested?"

In faro? No. In attending any gaming house with his friends? No. "Is it respectable?"

Francis nodded toward Harold. "Heard of it from Fairbanks."

Andrew nodded. Mr. Fairbanks was a mutual acquaintance of theirs from their years spent at school. The man was something of an idiot, but Andrew owned that he trusted the man's discretion. Fairbanks had too high an opinion of himself to step foot in a gaming house that would not pass muster.

Not that it mattered. Andrew had promised the evening to his sisters. To Mary.

"Perhaps another night, gentlemen."

"Ha!" Harold said, pushing to his feet. He held out a hand toward Francis as the man fished around his pocket and pulled out a coin, a wry smile on his lips as he dropped it in Harold's hand. The men exchanged money so often in bets and wagers that Andrew wondered if the same few coins moved back and forth each time.

"You wagered on my willingness to gamble?"

"On your willingness to come out with us," Francis clarified, annoyed. "I thought gambling was the way to win."

Harold took his seat again before leaning across the small table between their chairs and gripping Andrew's elbow. "And I knew there would be no way to pull you from your mother's house on Christmas. What does the old dragon have planned for the evening?"

"You call my mother a dragon again, and I'll see you out into the snow." Andrew pointed to the bubbled glass window at the end of the room, the fading sunlight making it appear orange. "Through that window."

"Forgive me," Harold said, though his amusement betrayed a lack of contrition.

"No special plans." Andrew swallowed against the lie. He wasn't about to tell his friends about the caroling puppet show. They would demand to remain in order to witness the spectacle, and he didn't want them ruining a nice family evening.

If he would have agreed to spend Christmas at Brightly Court like his mother had wished, they would have been able to go out together in search of a yule log—but things were different here. There was no convenient forest, only stalls from which to purchase things. And the more his mother was forced to sacrifice for this frosty London holiday, the more Andrew's guilt grew.

"Tomorrow, then?" Harold asked.

"I'm not sure what my mother has planned for tomorrow. If I am free, I will come in search of you."

Francis laughed, shaking his head, but Harold's face only grew serious. His eyes narrowed, regarding Andrew as though he could tell something was different but could not quite figure out what it was.

Andrew liked his friends, but he could not tell them of the turmoil that flew about him like a determined raven, pecking at him constantly. He couldn't explain that whenever he found some other thing to funnel his focus into, thoughts of Mary or his failure as his father's heir swooped in on him again, unrelenting.

If his good friend Alverton was nearby, Andrew would have been able to confide in him—to beg advice. But Alverton lived up north with his bride now. There was no one else in London he trusted to hear him unburden his fears and concerns, so Andrew was forced to turn to others for distraction. Though they had honorable intentions, that's all Harold and Francis were.

Perhaps he ought to visit Alverton when the snow melted, and the roads became passable. Harold and Francis *were* entertaining, but Andrew craved the steadying, reasonable nature of his closest friend.

"Be glad Almack's is not yet open, or I'm certain you'd be squiring your sisters there next," Francis said.

"They are not out yet," Andrew reminded them. "I have a year or two before that will be a concern. Except..." Hadn't Mary mentioned a Twelfth Night ball? Surely it would only be a small affair if Mother was going to allow Anne to attend.

"Yes?"

"Nothing. But I will do my duty by my sisters, whatever that may be. There is no one else to do it."

Harold nodded. He got to his feet, stretching his arms before him. "Well, if we cannot convince you to come along, I suppose we ought to go."

"You are welcome to stay," Andrew offered, his mouth going dry. He hoped they would deny the invitation. It had only been a formality.

"That sounds—"

"No," Harold said, cutting Francis off. "We don't wish to interrupt your evening. We'll be off."

Francis looked as though he was about to argue, but Andrew relaxed when he relented, following Harold from the room.

The blessed silence fell upon Andrew as he listened to his friends' footsteps trail down the stairs, out of the house, and onto the snowy London street. Melancholy descended on him, and he shut his eyes to the room, the crackling of the fire pulling a memory from his child-hood—his father, sitting near a fire and speaking to his mother about what they could do to help their uncle, who'd lost his fortune and had nowhere to turn. Mother had wanted to wait in the case that someone else would offer the man a place in their home, but Father had disagreed. He believed helping his uncle to create independence for himself would be most beneficial for the man in the long run.

Andrew had sat on the floor between their chairs, the fire roaring and spitting behind him as he played with small tin soldiers on the rug and listened to the points his father made. Even then he had noted how Father's wish was, above all, to help.

Such selflessness and humility were traits Andrew could never himself claim. He was not the giant of giving and kindness his father had been. He would never be the earl his father was.

"Oh, forgive me!"

Mary's voice pulled him from his melancholy musings as swiftly as if she had shaken him with her hands instead of her words. Opening his eyes, he found the woman standing across the room from him, her round eyes widened, her hand resting against the bookcase.

"I did not know you were here, my lord. We finished with the puppets and I only wanted to select a new book to read. I hadn't real-ized the room was occupied."

He'd heard those words before from other women, women who'd claimed to be innocent—*accidentally* stumbling upon him alone in a room. But this time he believed it. When Mary appeared to be looking for a book, he knew she was absolutely looking for a book.

The misfortune was that this time he almost wished she had come in here with malintent. He wouldn't mind being caught alone with her.

Shaking that inappropriate thought away, Andrew tried to smile. "You are forgiven, Miss Hatcher." He rose, dipping his head in acknowledgment. "Might I help you find something?"

"Perhaps. Though I will warn you, there aren't many books I haven't yet read."

So she was an avid reader? The idea did not surprise him. It filled him with a greater understanding of her character. "Consider this a challenge I will gladly accept."

Her mouth turned up, a slight chuckle escaping her lips. She pulled away from the bookcase. "Are you a well-read man?"

"I like to think so."

"Funny, I would have—"

Andrew waited for her to continue, but her lips remained closed, a blush staining her cheeks.

"Yes?" he pressed.

She shook her head.

Andrew crossed the room, coming to a stop just before her. He crossed his arms over his chest and leaned one shoulder against the bookcase on the wall. "You cannot blush so prettily and refuse to tell me why. It is unfair."

Her eyebrow arched, and she mimicked his position, a case of books separating them. "Are you suggesting that I am not allowed my secrets?"

"On the contrary. You may keep your secrets. I'm only begging to be admitted into your confidence."

The room dimmed along with the setting sun, but the firelight behind them and the lamps on the table glowed against Mary's face, making her green eyes shine. They reminded him of the jade stick pin his father used to wear in his cravat. The one that now sat in Andrew's dressing room upstairs.

He leaned closer and lowered his voice. "I promise, I am quite adept at keeping secrets, too."

She laughed. "You do realize that you just contradicted yourself, yes? You believe you can flash your smile at me, and I will reveal my uncharitable thoughts."

Uncharitable thoughts? What on earth had she meant to say when she stopped herself?

Andrew grinned. "But is it working?"

CHAPTER 8

*M*ary's breath caught. Lord Sanders watched her so intently, his smile so wide and genuine, that she found her heart pattering in her chest like rain against a tin roof. It was bold, loud in her own ears.

The troubling part was that his charm *was* working. She wanted to open her heart and tell him everything. When Lord Sanders looked at her, spoke to her, he gave her his full attention in a way she had never before experienced. She did not feel ornamental in his presence. She felt seen.

She tried to chuckle lightly, but the sound was off. She had stopped herself from saying something less than considerate about her first impressions of the earl. But if he was going to press her this much, he deserved to hear it. "It was nothing, my lord. I was going to make the observation that I would not have pegged you as a man who enjoyed reading."

He unfolded his arms, dropping his chin. "I'm wounded. You believe me to be dull?"

"Quite the opposite," she said.

Lord Sanders quirked an eyebrow. "I will take the compliment and concede you the win—"

"How gracious of you."

"—on the condition that you allow me to choose the next book you read."

"So long as you select a book I have not yet read, I will happily agree."

His smile widened, showing her a set of slightly uneven, white teeth. "I know just the one."

Andrew stepped around her, and she spun on her heel to watch him. His light brown eyebrows pulled together in concentration, small creases forming between them, as his eyes searched the book spines lining the wall. The firm set to his mouth gave his countenance a far more determined look than she was used to seeing on him, and she swallowed her mirth. He was taking this seriously.

"What is the book?"

"Around here somewhere," he muttered, his finger trailing the titles as he looked. He tapped one before pulling it from the shelf and turning it over in his hand to read the cover. Then he held it out to Mary. "I bought this set for Anne last year, but she isn't much of a reader. I am convinced she would love it were she to give it a try. It is the first of three volumes, and they are all on this shelf. If you enjoy it, you can return here for the next installment."

Mary read the title. *Pride & Prejudice*. That sounded far from promising. "And you believe I might enjoy it?"

Lord Sanders was silent. She glanced up to find the earl's gaze fixed on her, a furrow to his brow.

"Pardon me." He shook his head slightly. "I am unsure if you would enjoy it. But I am interested to find out."

Mary pulled the book against her, wrapping her hands over it. "Then I shall report back."

Lord Sanders's lips hitched in a smile. "I will anxiously await your thoughts."

The warmth from the fire reached Mary's back, spreading through her body and making the room grow smaller. Lord Sanders stood across from her, his hands casually clasped before him. He appeared at ease, comfortable, while her chest warmed from the kindness he'd shown her.

But she had seen his posture when she'd barged into the room earlier, completely unaware of his presence until it was too late. She'd seen the bend of his eyebrows, the frown on his lips, his eyes closed to the world as though he was doing his utmost to keep it away.

Would that she could ask him now of his troubles, that she could lend a listening ear.

"Are you prepared to sing the carols?" he asked, taking her by surprise. The way he'd been watching her had been so intent, she almost wondered if he'd been reading her thoughts, but his lips said otherwise.

"I know the songs, so I suppose I am as ready as can be expected."

"You do realize Anne will be listening closely to determine your level of skill as a singer."

Mary chuckled. She hadn't thought of that, but he was likely correct. "She will be disappointed. It is not a skill I possess."

Lord Sanders tilted his head, narrowing his eyes at her. "Are you being modest?"

"No. I am not." She laughed. "Trust me. I can blend into the congregation at church passably enough, but I cannot sing well."

"I suppose I shall find out soon."

Mary couldn't fight the grin spreading over her lips. "And now I am tempted to whisper so that neither of you will be able to hear me and claim the win."

"But you have more integrity than that," he said, as though this was a truth universally acknowledged.

It gave Mary pause. She had known *of* the Bright family her entire life, but she had only been on personal terms with them for the last few weeks —and Lord Sanders, mere days. She liked to think she had integrity too, but knew it to be false. If she had integrity, she never would have agreed to her father's idea to fulfill their side of the marriage bargain with Mr. Lockhart by obtaining an invitation to the Brights' summer house party.

Lord Sanders's clear, guileless blue eyes focused on Mary, causing her throat to tighten. She clutched the book to her chest, stepping back. If he knew her intentions, he would not think she had integrity.

"I must change for dinner," she said, stepping back further. "Thank you for the recommendation."

Lord Sanders dipped his head in a bow. "I hope it brings you pleasure."

"A book about pride and prejudice? I am curious to see how it might."

A knowing smile flitted over his lips, and Mary forced herself to look away. She turned, leaving the library, her heart in her throat. When Father had proposed the plan, Mary hadn't realized how foul it was going to feel to carry it out.

She hurried up to her room and set the book on the dressing table, turning to allow her maid to begin unfastening her gown.

"Thank you, Price," Mary said, slipping from the gown and waiting for her maid to set it down and lift her dinner dress. She had two gowns from which she could choose to dine in and had rotated between them both for the duration of her stay. She only hoped her limited selection had not been noticeable to her hostesses.

Sliding her hand through the long, green silk sleeve, her finger caught on a hole. The harsh sound of ripping fabric rent the air, threads breaking like a volley of nuts cracking as her finger tore down the seam.

"No!"

"It's all right, ma'am," Price said, bustling forward to take the dress. "I can mend it right quick."

"But you need to dress Mother, as well."

Price paused, holding the green gown in her hands, a kind smile creasing the sides of her eyes, her wrinkles becoming more pronounced. "I can do both."

Mary drew in a breath and reached for her gown. She and Mother shared Price as a lady's maid. Back home it wasn't much of a trial, as they dined early and had plenty of time to change. Mary had grown accustomed to preparing for dinner early so Mother could have Price as long as she needed. But even she could now see that there wasn't enough time for Price to dress mother, fix Mary's thoughtless tear, and complete her toilette.

"I will sew the tear. You see to Mama and then come back to me. If we do not have enough time to fix my hair, then this will have to do for tonight." She reached up and smoothed a tendril away from her forehead.

"But Miss Mary, it's Christmas."

Mary looked at the matronly maid sharply. "And we are to spend it with family. It is nothing of consequence if I am a little plain." She set her mouth in a firm line, hoping the maid would see her posture and understand her firm stance in this matter. "Now, go see to Mama."

"Yes, ma'am."

Price left the room, not pausing to glance back, and Mary retrieved her small sewing box from her trunk. Slipping her dressing gown over her underclothes, Mary nestled into the chair near the fire, the window dark now and the fire her only source of light.

She turned her wounded sleeve inside-out and found the tear. Preparing a needle, she got to work. She'd hoped that the extra time she would have had after dressing for dinner would have allowed her to begin the novel Lord Sanders had recommended. But alas, she would now have to wait until after dinner.

Her fingers worked as though they had a mind of their own, her thoughts trailing to the moment in the library when she'd come upon the earl. He'd been troubled, but when she spoke to him his demeanor had shifted completely. She did not have a high enough opinion of herself to imagine that speaking to her was the cause for such a shift. The man was clearly battling something within himself, and Mary would do well to put it from her mind completely.

It was none of her concern.

Perhaps if she repeated that to herself often enough, she would grow to believe it.

CHAPTER 9

$\mathcal{T}$he drawing room smelled of drying evergreen boughs and burning wood from the fire roaring in the hearth, crackling and spitting embers against the floral-painted firescreen. The mothers sat on a plush settee facing the long sofa which Lady Anne, Lady Caroline, Lord Sanders, and Mary crouched behind.

Nestled between the earl and his youngest sister, Mary pulled the stocking puppet further up her arm and smiled at Lady Caroline.

"I'll go first," Lady Anne whispered from the end. Everyone nodded and Lady Anne's slender arm raised above the sofa, her voice taking on a high, tinny quality she likely affected to bring humor to the show. "Ladies of the drawing room, we proudly present to you a performance by the Carolers of Sanders House."

Lord Sanders nudged Mary's elbow, and she glanced at him, his eyes sparkling with mischief. She prepared her puppet and lifted it at the same time Lord Sanders and Lady Caroline raised theirs to join Lady Anne's.

And then they began to sing.

Mary kept her voice soft, staying within the small range that her alto could manage well enough. They caroled, the songs of Christmas filling the room with warmth and joy. Lord Sanders's stocking strayed close to Mary's, his arm brushing against hers and resting there.

She shot him a glance and found him grinning, his smile wide despite his singing. His voice was pleasant, warm. Mary moved her arm away, but Lord Sanders followed. There was not a good deal of room behind the sofa as it was, and his antics were only making her space shrink.

"I did warn you about Andrew," Lady Caroline whispered when the song came to a close.

She had. But hadn't the earl claimed that he'd outgrown such antics? It made Mary smile.

They began the next song, and Lord Sanders moved further down the line of puppets, slipping his arm behind Mary's to pop up behind Lady Caroline's puppet. His forearm leaned against Mary's, but he hardly seemed to notice, his gaze over the top of Mary's head, watching his little sister giggle as she tried to escape the earl's theatrics. The smell of his shaving soap, clean and musky, washed over her in waves, making it difficult to remember words to the hymn, *While Shepherds Watch Their Flocks*.

By the time they finished the second song, Lord Sanders had crouched behind Mary where he could reach Lady Anne's puppet. The Bright girls were both giggling, fighting to sing through their mirth and leaving Mary to carry the bulk of the tune, to her utter displeasure.

When the carols came to a close, they all rose, bowing with their stockings and grinning at their mothers, who both smiled back with immense pleasure and amusement on their radiant faces.

"Lovely, darlings. Absolutely lovely!" Lady Sanders said, clapping her hands together.

"That was marvelous," Mama agreed.

Lady Anne turned to Mary. "I suppose I ought to have believed you, Mary. Your singing voice is no nightingale."

Mary laughed, the sound ripping from her chest. "Am I a screeching pig, then?"

"Of course not," Lord Sanders admonished. "And don't listen to my careless sister. I rather liked your voice."

Scrunching her nose, Mary turned to the earl. "Your manners are impeccable, sir. I won't do you the dishonor of calling you a liar to your face."

"You will merely think it instead?"

She closed her mouth, her smirk matching his, and pulled the puppet from her hand.

"Oh, Andrew!" Lady Caroline said, tugging on his sleeve, though his gaze remained on Mary. "We forgot to put together the servants' baskets for St. Stephen's Day."

"We may do so in the morning," he said, tearing his gaze away from Mary. She slipped away, moving around the sofa and taking the seat beside Lady Anne.

"Or we can do so now." Lady Anne removed her puppet and laid it over the arm of the sofa. "Is everything ready?"

"I believe so." He stepped around the sofa, pausing at the edge of the circle of furniture. Rubbing the back of his neck, his cheeks went rosy. "I am afraid the boxes won't be up to par this year, but I did my best. Mother is better at planning for these. I am certain the servants far prefer when she does so."

"I am certain the servants will love whatever you purchased for them, dear," Lady Sanders said.

"I suppose we will soon find out. Anne?"

She rose from the sofa and together they left the room, presumably to fetch the items he'd purchased for the servants' boxes. Mama leaned toward Lady Sanders, clutching her friend's arm as she spoke to her quietly.

"Do you miss your papa?" Lady Caroline asked, pulling Mary's gaze away from their mothers as she claimed her sister's empty seat.

Mary paused, unsure of how to answer the question. No, she did not miss her father at all. The time away from him and his high expectations had been a blessed holiday, and she found herself growing more eager for her wedding the longer she stayed away from her father. If nothing else, marriage to Mr. Lockhart was a blessing in that it would remove Mary from her father's household entirely. He was not a bad man, but he had expectations that she was tired of trying to reach.

"He is likely enjoying the respite," she said instead, careful to only speak the truth. "My father values quiet above all else, and with my mother and me here, I am certain he is getting enough quiet to heartily please him."

Lady Caroline's young face shifted in surprise. "Oh, but surely he misses you."

Lady Anne and the earl returned, saving Mary from needing to respond. She faced the door, watching them carry in crates—one full of small boxes and two precariously stacked in Lord Sanders's arms holding a multitude of items.

"You could have asked Finch to carry these," Lady Anne said.

"I am not asking our butler to carry his own gift," the earl replied.

"Mama, would you like to help?" Lady Anne called, setting her crate on the table nearest the window.

Lady Sanders shook her head. "No, dear. You go ahead."

Lady Anne nodded before turning her attention to the small boxes, lifting them from the crate and lining them up on the table to be filled with gifts for the servants. Mary moved to assist her and together they lined up the boxes until the tabletop was full, using two of the chairs to hold the last four.

Lord Sanders reached into one crate beside his feet and pulled out an orange. "Miss Hatcher, would you like to be in charge of placing the fruit in the boxes?"

Her breath caught. Could the man grow any more thoughtful? She nodded, reaching for the orange in his hands. He relinquished it to her, and she brought it up to her nose, sniffing the earthy citrus smell of the peel and allowing the feel of Christmas to wash over her body.

She was so satisfied, so happy in the Brights' home, she never wanted to leave it.

❄

Andrew watched Mary's eyes drift closed as she inhaled the scent of the orange. Her delicate fingers wrapped around the large fruit, his heart squeezing as though it was the orange Mary held. He turned away from her, trying to get his pulse under control as he sifted through the second crate and pulled out a sack of coins, tossing it to Caroline.

"Will you put two coins in each box?"

She nodded, and he turned back to retrieve the scarves.

"Andrew!" Anne squealed, beating him to it. She pulled a long, woolen scarf from the crate. "How did you manage to obtain these in so little time?"

"I found a woman on Bond Street who had almost enough already made," he said, shrugging. In truth, it had taken a good chunk of his day to locate the ready-made scarves, but he had been so cold while searching for the evergreen boughs for Anne that the thought occurred to him that his servants ought to be gifted something to aid them in this frightfully cold winter. "She was more than happy to make the last three that I needed and sent them over this morning."

"How exceptionally kind of you, my lord," Mary said, her eyes glowing in appreciation. "I am certain your servants will be prodigiously grateful."

"And yours," he said softly, earning a surprised look from Mary. He cleared his throat. "I inquired as to how many servants you brought to London and made certain your maid would be included." He gestured to the boxes. "You may take one this evening if you wish so you may present it to her in the morning."

Mary's mouth dropped open, her eyes widening. Her gaze flicked from the boxes lining the table to Andrew, and he had to force himself to remain where he was, to not look away from her penetrating gaze.

"That was thoughtful," Anne said, handing the first scarf to Mary. She stepped around her brother to pull out another.

Mary held up the one in her hands, peering at the workmanship. They were admittedly on the plain side, but they were thick and would be quite warm.

"Truly? She had all these at the ready?" Anne asked.

Her logical question pulled Andrew from the warm euphoria he had been in while under Mary's steady, grateful gaze, and he looked at his sister. "I imagine this shockingly cold winter gave her reason to believe she would sell a good amount of scarves. She also had extra gloves in her store and many hats. This is an extreme frost we are enduring, of course."

Anne nodded as though this logic made sense to her and returned to filling the boxes with scarves as Caroline dropped coins in them and Mary tucked oranges safely inside. Andrew busied himself with closing the boxes once they contained each of the three gifts and stacking them within the now empty crates.

The Bright siblings and Mary worked alongside one another, swiftly completing their tasks. There were two oranges left over, and they decided to peel both of them and share the segments, taking them to the sofas to offer pieces to their mothers. By the time the oranges were eaten, Andrew was quite drunk on joy and feminine laughter. Mary and her mother fit in well among the Bright family, and they shared a Christmas evening that was far better than any he'd had the last few years.

Last year's Christmas dinner had meant to be a bachelors' escape. Andrew and his friend, the Duke of Alverton, had escaped to his mother's empty estate in Wiltshire. But Alverton's family had arrived and ruined all plans for a quiet dinner. He hadn't been angry at his friend, but the stark contrast between last year's celebrations and this evening was vivid.

Andrew would choose this year's Christmas if given the choice again.

"I am exhausted," Mary said, rising from her seat on the sofa. "If you will all excuse me, I think I shall call it an early night." She yawned as if her body meant to prove her fatigue, and the rest of the party bid her goodnight. Andrew watched her leave with regret, wishing he could have spent more time speaking with her that evening. He loved having his sisters about, but he found he would greatly appreciate the opportunity to converse with *just* Mary.

Perhaps if he hung around the library long enough, he'd get his chance.

CHAPTER 10

*T*wo full days had passed since Christmas, and the occupants of Sanders House had fallen into a comfortable routine, sharing mealtimes and partaking in parlor games, with the afternoons unequivocally dedicated to quiet activities. Andrew's mother had gone upstairs for a nap, and her guest, Mrs. Hatcher, had done the same. Mary had taken a chair close to the fire, her feet tucked under her as she sat engrossed in the book in her hands, and Anne and Caroline were installed at the table beside the window, drawing.

Finch stepped into the library carrying a silver tray containing an ivory card and the *London Times* and presented them to Andrew. Andrew took the newspaper and tucked the card into his jacket pocket. He was not about to admit his friend into the room whilst Anne sat nearby—there was no predicting what his sister might do when faced with such a tantalizing treat. Not that Harold was a superb catch. But that likely mattered little to Anne. He was simply a man, which was more than enough qualification in her mind.

Andrew flicked his head, and Finch nodded in understanding. He would see Harold out kindly.

Andrew settled on the sofa opposite Mary, his back to his sisters as he pretended to read the newspaper. The articles with their bold titles ceased to grab his attention. The mention of a shipping company having lost two of its cargo ships was a shame, but Andrew could not read two sentences beyond the headline without his gaze straying from the paper to where Mary was reading across from him.

Judging by the progress she had made in her novel, she was nearing the halfway mark of the second volume, which meant she was just about halfway through *Pride & Prejudice* as a whole, and Andrew longed to inquire what she thought of it thus far. Her eyelashes fanned out over her cheeks, stark against her pale skin. The gentle slope of her nose was small and delicate, and he wondered if her children would have such sweet, petite noses as well.

Or would they take after Mr. Lockhart instead?

Mary's gaze flicked up, catching his and holding it, and Andrew froze. He was caught, transfixed as though he was a rabbit, and she, the hunter.

Her lips turned up at the ends. "I will not be able to finish this book with such a rapt audience, sir. I know you are eager to hear what I think but staring at me is no way to learn my thoughts."

Andrew chuckled, fighting the inclination to glance over his shoulder and discern whether or not his sisters were listening. What would they make of such a pronouncement? It was innocent, to say the least, but his sisters surely wouldn't need much to formulate conclusions of their own making. They chattered softly behind him, though, and he allowed that to put him at ease.

"I am curious by nature," he explained, though it was a paltry excuse. He hadn't been watching her out of curiosity. He'd been fixated on her because he had no other choice—he was drawn to Mary.

She closed the book, keeping her finger within the pages. "Perhaps I ought to read upstairs. Your curiosity is distracting."

"Will you remain if I promise to focus on my newspaper?"

She raised an eyebrow at him.

Andrew rubbed his chin. "What if I face the opposite direction?"

"That would certainly improve the situation."

He stood, crossing the ornate navy and cream rug and lowering himself in the wingback chair just an arm's length from Mary. Now he was close enough to smell her soft, floral aroma. Perhaps this hadn't been the best idea.

He settled into the seat, turning toward her, and her gentle smile settled over him like a warm blanket. "Now if I get distracted, my sisters will receive the brunt of my stare."

"Very well, my lord. I promise I will update you the moment I finish the book."

"But what do you think of it now?"

She glanced at the leather cover in her hands, running her fingers over the gold embossed spine. "Mr. Bennet is quite amusing. And I admit I am interested to learn what becomes of Jane Bennet."

"Jane? Not Eliza?"

"Well, both."

Straightening the newspaper in his hands, Andrew turned his focus to the article he'd been attempting to read for the last quarter-hour. He would much prefer something akin to *Pride and Prejudice*. There was nothing wrong with enjoying a decent novel now and again. Of course, he tended to indulge more than most gentlemen of his acquaintance. What would Mary think if she knew how often he read?

"What is it you are reading?" Mary asked, pulling his attention once again from the article about the sunken shipping line.

He set the paper on his knee. "Nothing remotely interesting. A few sunken boats loaded with cargo, but nothing—"

"Which boats?" she asked, straightening in her chair and lowering her feet to the floor. Her bow-shaped lips flattened, creases forming on her brow. Her concern was mighty, but the cause of it unclear. She did not have a stake in cargo ships, certainly. Her father was not a man of trade—he was a gentleman. A landowner.

Had he perhaps invested his money...but, no. The moment that thought entered Andrew's mind, he dashed it away. If Mr. Hatcher *did* have some stake in a shipping business, surely his daughter would be none the wiser.

What young gentlewoman took the least interest in her father's business dealings? The cause for her concern must be rooted elsewhere.

"The ships?" she prompted.

"Right," he said, scanning the article for pertinent information. "Fortescue Shipping ran into a hurricane outside of the Caribbean and lost two cargo ships to the sea."

Mary visibly relaxed, her finger slipping from the pages of the book and losing her place.

Andrew fixed his gaze on her careless finger, then watched her face for any discernible emotion. "Is there a shipping company you have a particular interest in, Miss Hatcher?"

She glanced up sharply. "Oh, of course you wouldn't know," she said, almost to herself. "Forgive me. I must have appeared quite the ninny. Mr. Lockhart owns a shipping company. He is presently returning to England on one of his ships."

A cool, thin band wrapped around Andrew's chest and tightened, but he did his best not to show his surprise on his face. Mr. Lockhart was a man of business? Andrew forced himself to meet her gaze, and the blush on her round cheeks struck him. Was she embarrassed about marrying into trade? Or merely because she had betrayed her sudden fear?

"You must forgive me," Andrew said. "I would never have mentioned the loss of a ship so casually had I known what the significance might be to you."

"You couldn't have known." She offered a kind smile. Sighing, she leaned her head back against the wingback chair. "And while Mr. Lockhart is safe, I can't help but mourn the loss of someone's ships. What a terrible blow that must have been."

Of course she would mourn the loss of a stranger's ships. It was a sad thing for someone's household, for someone's business, of course. But Andrew would not have thought twice of Fortescue Shipping without any personal stake in the outcome. No, had he been in Mary's situation, he would have felt merely relieved.

Mary reminded Andrew of his own father in that way. Father would have worried over a stranger's company. He was always asking after the needs of others, often staying late at church to discuss parishioners and how he might assist the vicar's efforts to relieve suffering for their people.

Andrew frowned. He'd never once stayed after church to see to the welfare of his people. He merely supplied the funds for others to do as much.

"Shall we play bullet pudding?" Caroline asked, skipping across the room with a wide grin on her face.

Mary sat up. "I am willing. It has been ages since I've played."

Andrew eyed his sister, shaking off the gloom which had settled upon him. "So long as I don't end up with a face full of flour, I will participate."

Caroline scrunched her nose. "That is not something I can promise, Andrew. You know it is entirely up to you."

"I was only teasing, Caro."

Caroline flicked him an arch glance before flouncing toward the fireplace and tugging on the bell rope. "I'll ask Finch to set it up straight away."

"I want to set the coin on top, though," Anne said, rising. "Mary, will you help me? We can go down to the kitchen and prepare the pudding ourselves."

"I'd love to." Mary rose and set the book carefully on the small table between their chairs. She looked up and caught Andrew's gaze, her jade eyes warm.

"I will come, too," Caroline said, joining the women near the door.

Andrew watched Mary follow his sisters from the room, her arm around Caroline as she leaned over to say something into the younger girl's ear. Caroline's laugh drifted from the stairwell as the women descended, and Andrew's chest warmed. Seeing his sisters happy was one of his utmost joys in life.

Knowing Mary was the cause of some of that happiness only sweetened her further.

"Andrew?" Anne stood in the doorway. She must have turned back. "Are you coming?"

"Absolutely."

Mary carefully lifted the overturned bowl from the wide plate, doing her best not to disturb the domed mound of flour left behind. She glanced at Lady Anne over the work-worn table. "Do you have the coin?"

Lady Anne produced a small halfpenny and placed it gently on top of the flour-cake, the King's stamped face looking over at Mary. Lady Anne glanced up at her sister. "You begin, Caro."

They all gathered around the end of the worktable, the chairs pushed to the side while the Brights' cook and kitchen maids bustled around behind them in the kitchen. The domineering fire in the over-sized hearth emitted waves of warmth, soothing away the chill seeping from the bare stone floor. Lord Sanders stood across from Mary, his sisters flanking him, their smiles easy.

Lady Caroline lifted a silver knife and sliced the edge of the cake as if being careful to avoid disturbing the coin sitting on top, though she was far from it. She handed the knife to her brother, and Lord Sanders did the same, cutting the very edge of the cake—so small a cut that it hardly warranted the name. A scrape would be more apt.

Mary had played this game a few times before but never had she seen such minuscule slices of the flour pudding. When the knife was passed her way, she took a thicker slice, though she was still far from the center of the mound, and in no danger of toppling the coin.

"You will lose quickly if you cut that way," Lady Anne said, her golden eyebrows rising on her forehead. A sudden grin spread over her lips. "Though I suppose I ought to be glad if it means *you'll* be digging in the flour with your nose."

"We shall see. No one is in danger yet," Mary said.

Lady Caroline took another turn, followed by Lord Sanders, then Lady Anne, all of them taking such tiny slices that Mary was uncertain they really could count. At this rate, they would be playing bullet pudding well into the evening.

As entertaining as this game could be, what she really wished to do was return to the comfortable chair beside the warm fire in the library and the novel awaiting her there. She needed to know what was going to happen to the Bennet sisters—to poor Jane and her beloved Mr. Bingley.

When the knife made it back to Mary, she poised it above the cake, then slid it closer to the coin before cutting her slice away.

Lady Caroline sucked in a gasp. "Are you *trying* to lose, Mary?"

"Of course not."

"Miss Hatcher is daring, Caro," Lord Sanders said, his voice dropping as though he feigned telling his sister a secret. "She wants to put us all to shame for our tiny slices."

"You mean your tiny scrapes?" Mary asked, sending Lord Sanders an arch look. "I don't believe those warrant being called a slice."

His booming laugh was sudden and warm, reaching over the bullet pudding and wrapping around her heart. She flushed with satisfaction, unable to dim her answering smile even if she wanted to. Which, she found, she did not.

"I can be daring, too," Lady Anne said, taking the knife from Mary and slicing the flour an inch wide. She offered her brother the knife with a smirk.

He took the knife, shaking his head. "I won't let Miss Hatcher influence the way I play."

"You will forever follow Father's example?"

Lord Sanders's eyes flashed. "He has not steered me wrong yet."

Mary caught the emotion which passed over the earl's face, quickly to be shuttered. "Was your father very cunning?"

"Oh, yes," Lady Anne said, her eyes wide in admiration. "He was smart, but he was fair. And he never lost at parlor games." Her nose scrunched up, her gaze seeking the ceiling in thought. "Well, he hardly ever lost."

This revelation about the late earl's nature was interesting, and Mary wanted to learn more about him, the man who had raised Lord Sanders and his delightful sisters. Lady Sanders was a good-natured, cheerful woman who didn't appear to want for anything and never had cause to exert herself in any manner. That her children grew up to be such playful creatures was likely due to her indulgent nature but could perhaps owe some credit to their father.

Lady Caroline took her turn and the flour that kept the halfpenny aloft slowly shrunk, each turn drawing the column thinner and thinner until Mary was left with a shaft of flour and no clear path to victory. She passed the knife between her hands, analyzing the flour from all angles.

"And here I assumed you did not care for winning," Lord Sanders said.

She ignored his remark, moving around the table to search for a better angle. Lady Caroline stepped out of her way. She came upon the earl, but he would not budge, and she could see why. From his side of the table, there was a place to cut that would, potentially, keep the coin from toppling.

"Excuse me, my lord."

"Yes?" he asked, as though he had no inkling that she was asking him to step aside.

His quizzical brow almost fooled her. She *almost* believed him to be in earnest. But his interest was too clear, his stance too solid.

"Would you mind stepping aside, my lord?"

"I am afraid I would mind, actually. Can you not cut from your own station?"

"I can if my intention is to lose."

He shrugged, which only lit the fire under Mary's desire to win. She stepped around Lord Sanders, but his arm flew to his sister, pulling Lady Anne tight against his side to create a larger barrier. Lady Anne giggled, remaining against her brother as Mary paused, hands on her hips, the dull knife clutched in her fingers.

She returned to Lord Sanders's vacant side and pressed against the table, leaning as far over as she could to reach the bullet pudding.

"Is this allowed?" Lady Anne asked.

"I suppose there are no rules prohibiting such leaning," Lord Sanders said, his voice low and amused.

Mary pressed against his side, steadying her arm as she positioned the knife. She brought it down on the flour carefully, doing her best to ignore Lord Sanders's warm body against her.

"Do not let the coin fall," Lord Sanders said suddenly, his voice sounding close to her ear.

Mary startled, feeling the earl's voice rumble through her shoulder where she pressed against him. The knife flinched in her hand and dashed sideways into the flour, toppling the coin onto the fallen pudding in a silent plunk.

Lady Caroline laughed, clapping her hands. "You nearly made it!"

Mary straightened, putting space between herself and the grinning earl. He stepped back, gesturing to his place at the table, that she might step into it if she wished.

"How chivalrous, my lord," she said wryly.

He dipped his head, accepting the compliment with a flourish.

Mary pulled the plate closer to her on the table. Tucking a brown curl behind her ear, she bent at the waist, closing her eyes and pushing her nose into the flour, searching for the coin.

Laughter from the Bright sisters echoed in the kitchen, and Mary dragged her nose around the flour until she nudged the cool, hard coin. Pressing her face further into the mound of white powder, she managed to get the coin between her lips and stood up triumphantly, blinking away the powder clinging to the fringes of her eyelashes.

Lady Anne laughed.

Lady Caroline stepped back. "You did it!"

Mary turned to Lord Sanders, but he stood back, the amusement absent from his face and replaced with warm admiration. Her heart stuttered, her pulse echoing loudly in her ears, and she turned back toward the plate, dropping the coin in the middle.

"Your face is white!" Lady Caroline said, laughing.

"Is it?" Mary asked, feigning confusion. "I wonder why. Perhaps it was this wretched flour." She dipped her hand into the pile on the plate and flicked it at Lady Caroline, who shrieked and ran to the other side of the kitchen, dodging around a surprised kitchen maid.

Mary dipped her hand again, and Lady Anne giggled, running behind her brother and clutching his arms.

"Does no one wish to match me?" Mary asked, a wide smile spreading over her mouth. Powder fell from her cheeks, and she tasted the gritty substance on her tongue, her nose wrinkling.

"Not particularly, no," Lord Sanders said.

Lady Anne peeked from around the earl's shoulder, and Mary dipped her other hand. Approaching the siblings, she lunged forward, reaching toward each of them at the same time. But Lady Anne ran away, and Lord Sanders did not move as Mary expected him to. She fell into the earl, her flour-laden hands pressing against his chest, and the soft rumble of his laugh vibrating against her palms.

Mary disentangled herself from his arms and glanced up to find two white handprints on Lord Sanders's coat over his chest. Her cheeks bloomed with heat—that was blessedly disguised by a white film—and she moved to wipe away the flour marks, only managing to smear the white powder further on his navy-blue coat.

"Don't trouble yourself," he said, gently grabbing her by the wrist and moving her hands away from his person.

"But your coat. I do hope I haven't ruined—"

"It is merely flour, Miss Hatcher. It will come right out."

His words were no balm against her embarrassment. Both of his sisters found the situation to be awfully funny, however, and their laughter filled the kitchen. The maids busied themselves behind them, one woman standing at the ready with a broom—likely to clean up after Mary's childish antics.

"Perhaps we ought to remove ourselves from the room and allow Cook full use of her kitchen once more," Lord Sanders said, sending the stout cook a wink. She grinned at him with patient indulgence, and his sisters obediently moved toward the stairs.

"I suppose it is nearly time to change for dinner," Mary said.

"For you, perhaps," Lady Anne called over her shoulder. "No one else changes quite as early as you do."

Maybe they were unaware that she shared a maid with her mother, but Mary was not about to inform them of that fact. They all mounted the stairs to the main floor, and Mary turned to continue up toward her room, Lord Sanders directly behind her, as his sisters left toward the drawing room.

When she shot him a quizzical glance, he smiled and indicated his flour handprints. "I figured I ought to change for dinner a little early tonight."

She laughed, hoping she appeared unrepentant. "It could have been avoided, had you not cheated, my lord."

His scoff followed her up the stairs. "That is a bold accusation."

"You don't admit to your attempt to rattle me?"

Lord Sanders smiled but failed to say anything more. Mary couldn't help the chuckle that began in her chest and rumbled forth as the earl walked away, leaving her standing in the corridor outside her door.

She watched his retreating form, his broad shoulders straight and proud. Mary slipped into her room and crossed to the looking glass, a grin spreading over her white powder-covered face. She laughed at the absurd picture she made. She hadn't felt so free, so silly, in years.

And she loved it.

CHAPTER 11

$\mathcal{T}$he window coverings were pulled tight, shut against the night, but Mary could easily imagine how dark the world was beyond the thick, damask drapes. She shrugged her arms into her thin dressing gown, tying the sash at her waist and tugging at her frayed sleeves. Her plait had started to come undone, and she ran her fingers over the ribs and edges of her hair, contemplating taking the ribbon off the end and re-plaiting it, but a swift glance at the clock reminded her that it was well past two in the morning, and she would not see anyone about the house so late.

She shouldn't be walking about the house so late, but she had just finished the second volume of *Pride & Prejudice* and she *needed* to get her hands on the third to learn what happened next. Elizabeth Bennet was on her way to an empty Pemberley, and Mary had a feeling she was going to love reading about the large house in Derbyshire.

She couldn't imagine being so rich. Swallowing against the thickness that built in her throat, she realized that in just a few short weeks she wouldn't need to imagine it—she would be wealthy. Marriage into the Lockhart family with their multitude of successful investments and an enormous shipping company was going to completely change her circumstances and her life.

She knew this marriage was nothing more than a business arrangement. There was no affection between herself and Mr. Lockhart. Neither of them had ever pretended otherwise. But he was a handsome man with a sound mind and marrying him was going to save her family's estate from ruin. Their arrangement already had.

Slipping into the corridor, Mary held her candle out and closed the door silently behind her. The quiet house felt empty, its lack of movement and noise equally eerie and comforting. She was glad not to see anyone while walking around in her nightclothes. The orange glow from her candle created a round halo of light, showing her enough of the stairs that she wouldn't misstep, but leaving the rest of the house dark beyond it.

The library was dark, and she stepped quietly across the carpet, searching the multitude of bookshelves for the one containing the first and third volumes of *Pride & Prejudice*. Her eyes lit on the matching burgundy spines, and she slipped the second volume into the middle spot before retrieving the third. It was going to take quite a lot of self-control not to light an additional candle and stay awake all night to finish the book.

Perhaps only a chapter tonight. She could force herself to close the book and go to sleep after one chapter, surely...

A soft snore sounded in the room, and Mary paused halfway to the door, standing on the carpet in the center of the room. She felt no warmth from the banked fire behind her, but she clearly wasn't alone. The hair on the back of her neck rose with the sound of another snore.

Someone was in this room, and they were sleeping.

Lifting the candle so she could better see, Mary turned around. Her eyes fell upon the earl, stretched out over the long sofa, his arm raised and forearm resting over his eyes. Lips parted, he breathed out another soft snore. She stood two paces away, watching the slow, steady rise and fall of his slumbering chest.

Clutching the book to her middle, Mary watched Lord Sanders sleep. Her body told her to turn and flee, to return to her bedchamber and pretend she hadn't come upon him. But her conscience urged her otherwise.

How could she leave the man to an uncomfortable night's sleep on this sofa when he had an empty bed just upstairs? Resolved in her decision, she moved forward, pausing when the light hit upon a brown leather rectangle on his chest.

A book. Lord Sanders had fallen asleep on the sofa *reading*. Never had a man been so attractive to Mary than in this moment.

Shaking away the wildly inappropriate thought, Mary cleared her throat loudly and waited.

Lord Sanders didn't stir.

Stepping forward, she leaned closer.

"Lord Sanders?"

Still nothing.

Setting her book on the small table at the end of the sofa, Mary reached for Lord Sanders's arm and nudged him gently. "My lord? Wake up."

His snores disappeared, his mouth closing at once as his body moved slightly. Mary stepped back, suddenly aware of their solitude. She was completely alone, in the middle of the night, wearing her nightclothes, with a man she hardly knew.

No, that was unfair. She might not have known him long, but she knew Lord Sanders's character. He wore it on his sleeve for all the world to see.

But still, perhaps she had time to escape before the earl discovered who had woken him.

"Yes?" The deep, groggy voice asked, his arm remaining over his eyes.

She crept across the carpet, making it nearly to the door when she realized she'd forgotten the book she'd come down for. Swiveling, she took one step back toward the little table and froze. Lord Sanders was sitting up, his tired eyes resting on her.

He'd shed his coat at some point and discarded his cravat. His shirt was open at the throat, a shadow lining the groove that ran the visible length of his collar bone.

"Were you trying to sneak away?"

Mary swallowed hard. "I was hoping to sneak out before you'd gained consciousness, my lord."

He regarded her steadily, a firm set to his mouth. Was he struggling to believe her?

She took a step closer, desperate to plead her case. "I only wanted to wake you so you might remove upstairs. It would not do to have a crick in your neck from sleeping on a sofa. I did not intend to speak to you."

His gaze dropped to her dressing gown, and she pulled it tighter, clutching it at the neck.

"I believe you." He scrubbed a hand over his face. "But what are you doing here at this hour?"

She gestured to the book on the table and he reached for it, a smile curving his lips. "You enjoy it, then? I'm glad."

"So far, yes."

He lifted it toward her, and she crossed the rest of the room to take the book from his hand, holding it against her middle. "What are you reading?"

"You are not allowed to mock me if I tell you," he said, one eyebrow lifting.

"I solemnly promise not to mock you."

"Byron."

"Poetry?" Her eyebrows lifted, and a smile came to her lips. "I was unaware you were interested in things like poetry."

"I am interested in a lot of things like poetry," he said, a challenge in his words. "Is it wrong of me? Do you believe poetry to be a language for women?"

"Not in the least. Byron is a man, is he not? As is Shakespeare, and I've heard it argued that the Bard is the king of poetry."

"Because of his turn of phrase, or the themes of which he wrote?"

"The structure of his writing, I should think." Mary backed into the soft wingback chair and lowered herself on the seat, resting her wrist against her knees so the light from her candle might still reach Lord Sanders's face. "While I admit to enjoying a few of his stories, I do not love them as much as I enjoy novels like this one." She laid her hand over the book in her lap.

"You are a reader for sport then, I assume, and not for knowledge?"

She held his gaze, his eyes sparkling, reflecting the flickering flame of her candle. "I believe all reading has its uses. But yes, I most enjoy reading for sport. Though I've never heard it referred to in such a way. How original."

His boyish grin spread wide. "So original that I might presume to call myself clever?"

Mary chuckled. "That is yet to be determined, my lord. But your affinity for reading"—she nodded to the book he'd set on the cushion beside him—"and poetry, specifically, leads me to believe you must be clever, indeed."

"Then I will be careful not to blemish that opinion with reality." His smile slipped, and he cleared his throat. "Your Mr. Lockhart, is he a lover of reading?"

Mary's hand tightened on the book in her lap. "I am unsure. To be honest, I don't know much about him. We were not very well acquainted before he left for India."

The look on Lord Sanders's face was difficult to decipher. She wanted badly to know what was happening in his mind, to learn what he was thinking. So, she continued, hoping he would reveal his thoughts through his expression. "Mr. Lockhart is a wealthy merchant, as I believe I already told you. He is unlike the men of my acquaintance—always busy with one important matter or another."

"And we gentlemen of leisure are not busy with important matters?"

A blush rose on her cheeks, warming them considerably; she hoped the glow from the single candle was not bright enough to reveal her embarrassment. "No, only that you are not quite so...so actively engaged. Though I suppose you are always going somewhere, are you not? To hunt, to fish, to ride...when in Town, you are always leaving for the club, or to play cards, or to see a man about something dreadfully dull."

"Dreadfully dull like horses and things?"

"Exactly. But there is no sense of urgency about you, not like the sort Mr. Lockhart carries with him."

"Will that not bother you?"

Her head reared back. "Heavens, no. I should think I will enjoy being left to my own devices more often than not."

He peered at her for so long, she was convinced he would say nothing more. But then he opened his mouth, his face still unreadable as stone. "More time for reading?"

Her lips bent in a smile. "Indeed. Much more time for reading."

"And I, on the other hand, don't have nearly enough time for it. I'm too busy heading to my club, playing cards, and seeing men about dreadfully dull horses."

Mary laughed. "You deny it?"

The smile which crossed over Lord Sanders's face was breathtakingly handsome, etching deep grooves on the sides of his mouth and crinkling the corners of his eyes. "Not in the least. You've quite painted my life in a concise picture. It is cause for introspection, actually. Though, that terrifies me."

"Why is that?"

The library became so quiet, Mary almost felt like she could hear Lord Sanders's breathing from across the rug.

"Because I have put it off for years, Miss Hatcher. I am quite afraid of what I will find if I look too closely at myself."

That saddened her, and she longed to reassure him in some way, though she did not know how to accomplish it. Did he truly think so low of himself?

"From what I have heard, your father was a good man. Surely—"

"I am nothing like him," he said, quiet but resolute. He lifted his face to meet hers. "If I could be half the man my father was, I would stand proud. But as it is...there is no value in trying. Even half as good is an impossible goal."

"Why do you say that? Surely he was not such a paragon. All of us have faults."

"He was as close as he could be. Not like me. I am too foolish, and not serious enough." He rested a hand on the volume of poetry beside him on the sofa. "I find value in reading for pleasure and spend too much time partaking in senseless wagers. Did you know I once raced my phaeton across London for a shilling? If that is not foolhardy, I don't know what is. Any number of things could have gone terribly wrong."

"Did your father disapprove of wagers?"

"Oh, mightily. But that never stopped me." He rubbed the back of his neck. "And he put my mother before all things. He doted on his daughters, on his people. I used to follow him around our estate like a loyal puppy. I once watched him climb upon a tenant roof *himself* to repair a thatch."

"He sounds like the sort of earl any man would be good to emulate."

"But that is my struggle," Lord Sanders said, and the pain in his voice tore at Mary's chest. "I could never emulate him. I am a wisp of his shadow, nothing more."

Heavy silence sat thick between them as Mary tried to determine how she might argue his point. If only she could show Lord Sanders a looking glass that reflected the way his sisters saw him, the way *she* saw him, perhaps he might—

Lord Sanders rose, leaving behind the book of Byron's poems. "It is really very late, I am guessing."

"Past two."

His eyebrows rose. "I am impressed, madam."

"With my lack of ability to control myself? I ought to have put the book down hours ago. And I really ought to go outside more often. I miss the sun."

He gave her a knowing smile. "As do I. The weather has been beastly cold, but the sun has shone the last few days."

"Perhaps we ought to…" She paused, realizing it was in no way her place to suggest any outings to the earl. He was such a gentleman, he would no doubt agree to anything she put before him. His eagerness to obtain evergreen boughs for his sister and oranges for Mary was proof of that.

"Yes?"

"No, my lord. Forget I said anything."

He gave her an apologetic smile, but she saw the telling glimmer of interest in his eyes. "I'm afraid I don't know how. You'll just have to tell me."

She stood, holding her book to her stomach as her other hand balanced the candleholder. "It is nothing. Truly."

"My curiosity knows no bounds." He stepped forward, her candle sending light over his open shirt and highlighting his neck as he swallowed. "I will lie awake in bed wondering what it is you were going to say."

"You cannot lay the blame for your own curiosity at my feet."

"You're right. That was unfair of me." He paused. "But I still would like to know."

She lifted her chin. "But if I tell you, you will make it happen. You are a gentleman of the highest order."

He looked ready to argue that fact, his eyes hardening. "I make no such guarantees if it will induce you to reveal yourself. Please tell me."

Mary sighed. "I was merely going to suggest an outing. A walk in the park or a ride in your mother's barouche. It is nothing, though, and I should have brought the idea to your sister instead."

"Anne would love the suggestion, I'm certain."

"Goodnight, my lord."

"No, wait," he said, reaching for her as she turned to go.

She paused. "I forgot. You don't have a candle, do you?"

"I don't...that is not...will you please stop calling me *my lord*?"

She stilled, stunned. "What else am I supposed to call you?"

"My name is Andrew."

Mary was unsure of what to say. She was engaged to another man. To take such liberties with Lord Sanders didn't feel appropriate.

"It is just that everyone else in this house calls me Andrew. My sisters, my mother."

Ah, that was it. He must think of her as a sister. It was a deflating, cooling thought. And *very* welcome. This was precisely how he should look at her. It was far more appropriate than how she thought of him, and she would do well to follow his good example. "I could, but I wonder what your sisters would think of it."

"Do not use my given name in front of them, then. You can merely drop the *my lord,* and I will be satisfied. No, not just satisfied. Immensely grateful. The reminder is so constant. I have been given these shoes to fill and I just…would you do this for me?"

"Yes, Andrew. I can do this for you."

"Thank you, Mary."

She held his smile, gripping her book so tightly, she was certain her knuckles were white. No man had ever called her Mary besides her father, and it sent a thrill through her.

This was the exact opposite of what she should feel right now, and she needed to get a better handle on her feelings, and soon.

CHAPTER 12

*A*nne stood at the window, staring wistfully out at the snow-covered street lit by the mid-morning sun. The drawing room was empty but for Andrew and his sister, and he was hoping she would be receptive to the idea he was about to propose. Well, it was Mary's idea, but it had been a good one. They had all been cooped up in the house for too long now.

While it felt like Mary was a beacon of light anytime she was in the room, *actual* sunlight would no doubt benefit them all.

"How would you feel about an outing to Gunter's for some chocolate?"

Anne spun on her heel, her smile radiant. "Andrew, do you mean it? Oh, when?"

"As soon as it can be arranged. I was hoping Mother would be amenable to the scheme, so we ought to go prior to her nap."

Anne threw her arms around Andrew's neck, stunning him. He froze for a moment, surprised, before he returned the embrace. Could Anne not see that he was trying to buy her affection? He supposed he ought to simply appreciate her gratitude and take his wins where he could get them.

Anne released him, grinning. "I will tell Mary and Caro right away."

"And I will speak to Mother."

He followed her from the drawing room and up the stairs to where the rest of the women of the house had remained within their bedchambers. Mary was usually awake and downstairs with Anne by now, but Andrew assumed her late morning was due to the late evening she'd had the night before. He still could not believe he'd had the gumption to ask her to call him by his Christian name, or that she'd agreed to. It was inappropriate, but he had wanted to hear it so badly, and the cover of darkness had emboldened him. But he knew he could never ask her for another thing. It was not behavior befitting a gentleman.

But who was he kidding? He was no gentleman. And despite her claims that she thought him—what was it she had said? Ah, yes—a gentleman of the highest order, he was anything but. Had he not said so when he revealed his insecurities about never living up to the man his father was?

Well, he'd established his lack of gallantry by calling her by her Christian name without her permission. She hadn't seemed to mind, but he knew better regardless of her graciousness. He wouldn't do it again without her consent.

Bringing up his fist, he rapped his knuckles on his mother's dressing room door and waited for her to bid him entry. He stepped inside, surprised to find Mrs. Hatcher seated on the settee near the fire while his mother was at the dressing table, her maid pinning long, gray curls into place.

"Good morning, Mother. Mrs. Hatcher." He bowed to each of them and received warm smiles in return.

"I was just telling Fanny of the new roofs you ordered for the tenants of Brightly Court. It was such a kindness, and I am certain they will be grateful for the added warmth."

"They likely would have appreciated it more had I ordered the roofs to be put in *before* winter was upon us, of course," he said wryly, avoiding Mrs. Hatcher's gaze. Mother had no business making him sound thoughtful. If his father was still around, he would have ordered the roofs done at the beginning of the summer. No, he wouldn't have ordered the roofs done at all...he would have done them himself.

"Oh, Andrew—"

"I was actually coming to see if you would like to accompany me on an outing to Gunter's?" He turned to Mrs. Hatcher. "I've heard good things about their chocolate. Or they have tea, of course. Or coffee."

"A cup of warm chocolate sounds delightful," Mrs. Hatcher said. "But I'm not sure my old bones would fancy a ride in the cold. I'm afraid you'll have to go without me."

Her old bones? Mrs. Hatcher could not be above fifty years of age, surely. He turned toward his mother. "Mama?"

"I will stay with Fanny, dear. I'm certain Mrs. Burne can make us a cup here."

"If you insist." Andrew hesitated, watching his mother's maid place a lace cap over her curls and pin it into place. There was something different about his mother, but he couldn't quite put his finger on what it was. Her hair was grayer, maybe? Or perhaps those wrinkles on her face had multiplied.

He refrained from scoffing, though just barely. What a wretched son he was, that his mother was aging before his eyes and he continued to make himself as absent as possible. His father would be disgusted if he was around to witness Andrew's neglectful behavior.

He needed to leave the room, and now.

"Andrew?"

Pausing at the door, he looked back over his shoulder.

"Thank you for spending time with your sisters. You know how they adore you, and we simply don't see you often enough. It means the world to me."

It was as if Mother knew how to take the dagger residing in his heart and twist it just so in order to cause pain of the acutest kind. He forced a smile. She couldn't know, or she would have refrained from saying anything.

After a quick bow to both ladies, he closed the door behind him and moved away from his mother's room with long, sure strides. He flew down the stairs, one set after another until he finally reached the ground floor and found his sisters waiting there, but there was no sign of Mary. He wanted to ask if Mary had denied the outing like her mother had, but he needed to catch his breath first.

Taking the stairs so rapidly had risen his heart rate, but not enough to rid his mind of the undeserving gratitude his mother bestowed on him. He wouldn't mind a bruising ride right now or a bout of fisticuffs, but the quick jog down the stairs would have to do for the present.

"Are you ready to go?" he asked Anne as she bent to Caroline, fastening their younger sister's pelisse.

"In just a moment," Anne muttered. She glanced up, her blue eyes reminding Andrew so much of their father's. "Mary should be down any moment."

Relief flooded his body. He would have been happy to spend the morning with just his sisters, but he was glad to have Mary along. The room always seemed brighter when she was in it.

As if his thoughts called her forth, she stepped down the stairs, a pelisse wrapped around her shoulders, as she tied her bonnet ribbons under her chin. A faint blush spread over her cheeks, and she dipped her chin, her dark lashes lowering.

Was she agitated because they had run into one another in the library the night before? An image flashed before his eyes of Mary wearing her green silk dressing gown, her long, brown braid resting over her shoulder while her slender fingers curled around the candle-holder. She'd looked so simple and beautiful then, and she looked lovely now.

This Lockhart fellow was a lucky man.

"Shall we?" Andrew said, opening the door and holding it for the women. They filed outside and down the stone steps to the carriage waiting for them on the street. After handing the women inside the carriage, Andrew followed them in, taking the rear-facing seat opposite Mary. "I wanted to take you all out in a barouche, but I'm afraid it is too cold for it today."

"Heavens, Andrew. We'd have frozen," Anne said, her eyes wide.

"Precisely why I did not continue with that plan." He shot Mary a glance, and her lips curved into a smile. "I had the thought that maybe the sun would be worth the cold. But alas, we can't drink our chocolate if our limbs won't move."

Caroline grinned up at Andrew. He held her gaze with difficulty until a moment passed, and he glanced out the window. He could not be the father figure she needed in her life. But he could be the brother she needed—or so he hoped.

They arrived at Gunter's, found an empty table inside the shop, and ordered four hot cups of chocolate and one package of peppermint-scented icing-sugar drops. Tucked into the corner at a small table, they sat sipping their delicious drinks and enjoying the sunlit scenery—a refreshing alternative to the walls and bubbled glass windows of Sanders House.

"I would have gladly escorted you all around Berkeley Square if it was not so dreadfully cold outside," Andrew said. "Perhaps we can take a short walk before we return home."

A jingle sounded through the small shop as the door opened, bringing a gust of bitter, cold air along with the couple that entered.

"Or perhaps not," Anne said, her small nose wrinkling.

"What's a little chill for a nice walk outside?" Andrew argued. "We will warm up quickly enough with fires and blankets when we return home."

"Perhaps if it is only a short walk," Mary added, "it won't be very terrible?"

"Miss Hatcher?" a man said, pausing just before their table and staring down at Mary, stunned as though he'd found his maid wearing trousers. His sleek, dark eyebrows had risen on his forehead, and his hand clutched an ebony walking stick—not that he appeared to be relying on it. He looked healthy, not much older than Andrew himself, and was dressed in such elaboration that the stick could be nothing more than an affectation.

"Oh, goodness," Mary said, her voice small and laced with surprise. Her round, green eyes had grown to the size of peppermints, her shocked eyebrows matching the gentleman's.

Andrew cleared his throat. "Is anything the matter?"

"The matter? No. Heavens," she said, attempting to rise before appearing to realize that she was very much pushed into a corner. Reclaiming her seat, she said, "Lord Sanders, Lady Anne, Lady Caroline, allow me to present to you, Mr. Lockhart."

Anne let out a muffled squeal and Caroline a small gasp, but Andrew found he could elicit no response. The dandy's face had fallen into something between a bored expression and a proud smirk, and he bowed.

"Mr. Lockhart, these are the friends my mother and I are staying with in Town."

His eyes lit at once, settling on Andrew with an eagerness about them. He stepped closer. "How good of you to care for Miss Hatcher and her mother. I am inordinately grateful, my lord."

"It is nothing," Andrew said with a flick of his wrist. He had been brought up an earl, and though his father was never one to exhibit haughty behavior, he had known how to command a room when he wished, and Andrew had studied that art immensely as a young boy. He merely hoped he was doing it well enough now that he did not appear an inexperienced goose.

"Mary has been such a dear friend," Anne said, her excitement nearly palpable.

What would this man think of being addressed by a veritable child?

Mr. Lockhart smiled briefly, and Andrew had to grant the man a little gratitude for not putting her off completely.

These dandyish men-about-town could never be trusted to consider others more than they did their own toilette. Perhaps Andrew had misjudged Mr. Lockhart. Well, there was only one way to truly tell—he needed to spend more time with the man.

"Are you planning to stay in Town long?" Andrew asked.

"Yes," Mr. Lockhart said, drawing an ornate snuffbox from his pocket and flicking it open with one finger. He took a pinch and shut the box with a snap before returning it to his pocket. "At least until this blasted weather lets up. We nearly didn't make it *into* town. Traveling clear to Berkshire would be impossible at this point."

Mary didn't flinch at Mr. Lockhart's foul language. Her tone betrayed more anxiousness than anything else, and Andrew wanted to discover the cause of her concern. "I was unaware that you were planning to come to London," Mary said. "If I'd known, Mother could have—"

"Do not trouble yourself, Miss Hatcher. I'm putting up at the Clarendon."

"Would you and your party care to dine with us tomorrow?" Andrew offered.

"No party," Mr. Lockhart said. "I've come alone."

"Forgive me. When you said *we* nearly didn't make it into Town, I made an assumption."

Mr. Lockhart stared at Andrew for a moment, confusion resting on his eyebrows before his face slid into a pleasant smile. "I came in on the stage, of course. And I was not the only passenger."

Andrew nodded, but his gut clenched. Something was most certainly off about Mr. Lockhart's explanation, though Andrew could not put a finger on precisely what it could be. "Tomorrow then?"

"Tomorrow," Mr. Lockhart agreed, then turned to Mary. "And I quite look forward to speaking to you." His gaze rested on her a moment longer than was typically acceptable, before he bowed to the table, turned, and left the tea shop.

"That was odd," Mary said, her fingers playing with the cord of her reticule in her lap. Her soft brown eyebrows were drawn together, her lips slightly pursed.

Andrew itched to reach for her, to place a reassuring hand on her arm, but he held back. "I daresay he was the last man you expected to see today."

She chuckled. "Yes, of course. But what was even odder was that he did not purchase anything. He came in, spoke to us, and left."

"Perhaps the sight of you caused him to forget why he ever stepped foot in here in the first place," Anne said with a dreamy sigh.

"Or more likely, he saw you from outside and came in to greet you," Caroline offered. Of course the youngest of their party would have the most reasonable explanation.

Mary watched the woman who stood alone at the counter before she swept her gaze toward Caroline and smiled. "You are likely correct. I'm sure that was it."

But Andrew was not. As the women returned their attention to their drinks, he considered the entire situation from every possible angle. Something did not quite fit, and Andrew was determined to figure out what it was.

CHAPTER 13

*M*ary clasped the ruby earrings on her earlobes, twisting the backs until they tightened just enough to stay put. Her maid, Price, continued to pin curls high on her head, forming what she hoped would be an elegant coiffure. Mr. Lockhart was coming to dine, and Mary needed everything to be perfect.

Father was depending on her.

Price pulled the old, pale green ribbon from the table and strung it through Mary's hair, tucking the ends into the folds of her curls. She stepped back, clasping her hands before her and nodding.

Mary tilted her head to the side, faintly touching the base of her gathered curls. "Thank you, Price. It is quite lovely."

She had not expected the first time she saw Mr. Lockhart again after such a distance to be in a public tea room with a table of chocolate cups and her hosts between them. His skin was darker than she remembered—a likely result of the long journey he'd just sustained—and his eyes were brighter, his hair longer. He was just as handsome and courteous as she recalled.

But appearances aside, seeing Mr. Lockhart in the flesh had given her anxiety of the acutest kind.

Not only had the man been real, flesh and blood standing before her, but he was going to *marry* her. The last time she'd seen Mr. Lockhart, marriage was still an abstract reality, something far away that she would have plenty of time to come to terms with. Now, her upcoming marriage stared her in the face.

"If that's all, ma'am?"

"Yes, Price, that is all. You may go see to my mother."

Price dipped her white-capped head and scurried from the room. It was unfair to require so much of the maid; she not only had to see to all the mending, washing, and caring for both Mary and Mama, but also needed to dress them both and manage their hair. The first thing Mary planned to do when the vows were complete was hire a new lady's maid and leave Price to her mother and half the work she was presently enduring.

One last look in the mirror, and Mary smoothed her ivory gown, tugging at the sage green overlay. She picked up her long, ivory gloves and left the room, pulling them into place as she descended the stairs.

She had one hour before she would need to place herself in the drawing room to await Mr. Lockhart, and she planned to spend that time in a book.

The house was quiet and calm, as the rest of the women were sequestered in their rooms preparing for dinner. Mary let herself into the library, crossing the room to where she had left her book the evening before on the small table beside the wingback chair, and pulled up short when her eyes lit upon the earl seated on the sofa opposite.

He stood, offering her a bow. "Good evening, madam."

"My lord." She dipped her head, pausing before the chair. "I only came to retrieve my book. I shan't bother you."

"You are no bother." He looked pointedly at her, his hands lazily clasped behind his back. His coat was black, striking against his bronze waistcoat and a crisp, white cravat. He appeared at ease but resolute, his posture unbending, steadfast. He gestured to the seat she had meant to occupy.

"I am nearly finished with the book," she said, hoping he would take that to understand that she would not remain in his library for very long.

"Good, good." He waited for Mary to be seated before he followed suit. "And what do you make of it thus far?"

"Can we not wait until I've read the final thirty pages before we discuss it?"

"I am eager to hear your opinions."

She wanted to ask why he cared for her opinion at all, but it felt an impertinent question. The man was, more likely than not, only doing his best to be a kind host, to engage her in conversation for the sake of politeness. There was no other explanation; he simply had a kind heart, which she knew from watching him with his family, from witnessing the way he served them.

"I am hopeful the story will come to a happy end, but I haven't quite reached that point."

"And Miss Eliza Bennet? What do you make of her?"

He watched her so closely, Mary wanted to shrink away. What was he hoping to learn from such a pointed stare? "I believe she fell in love with a man who she once rejected, and now fears all hope is lost."

"Fell in love with a *man*, or with his house?"

"His house, of course," Mary said, unable to hold back her smile.

But Lord Sanders was not smiling. He held her gaze in his like a steel trap.

"I said that in jest," she explained, her voice soft. "Of course Elizabeth Bennet has fallen in love with the man himself. I believe her reference to loving Pemberley to be a sarcastic one."

"I would like to believe the same."

"Then do believe it. It is fiction, is it not? Unrealistic and lovely, of course, but not a factual story. You may believe whatever you wish."

Lord Sanders's face grew wary, concerned. "Why is it relevant that the book is fiction? Do you not believe it could be possible for a woman to fall in love with such a prideful, rich man in reality? To love him despite his riches?"

"I do. And I do believe a man could fall in love with a prideful young woman, as well. But when one considers the various relationships in this story, as far as I have read, at least, is not Mr. Collins's marriage to Miss Charlotte Lucas the more realistic? He is certainly not the rich, handsome bachelor, and though he may be silly, he is a decent man with a good situation."

"You believe it is better to marry for convenience's sake than to marry for love?"

"Love is good for stories," she said, lifting the book in her lap, "but it is unrealistic when pitted against the realities of life. I'm certain there are those with the luxury to make such a match, but it is surely as uncommon as finding a man like Mr. Darcy in the wilds of the countryside."

Lord Sanders looked struck. He opened his mouth, but then closed it again as if deciding against speaking. After clearing his throat, he seemed to collect himself. "Do you mean to say that you are not marrying for love?"

Mary drew in a sharp intake of breath. Had her position not already been made perfectly clear? He could not honestly expect her to answer. "That is an impudent question, my lord."

"Have I not asked you to call me Andrew?"

She shook her head. "I never should have taken such a liberty. It is far from appropriate, and I believe you know that. I cannot do such a thing when you are neither my brother nor my betrothed. Please don't ask it of me again."

He nodded, his eyes growing hard. "I understand. Forgive me. I have been lulled these last few days into feeling as though we've been acquainted longer than we actually have."

Mary could say nothing in response to this. She understood him, for she felt very much the same. Perhaps it was a product of spending so many hours together in the day, so many days in a row, but she felt like she knew Lord Sanders better than she knew most people of her acquaintance. She certainly felt she knew him better than she knew Mr. Lockhart.

But that was irrelevant. Shaking the thought away, she pasted a smile on her face. "Love is not a lasting, tangible necessity. It is nothing when compared to the contentment that comfort can bring."

"By comfort, do you mean a fortune?"

Mary's cheeks warmed. She stood, clutching the book with tightened fingers. She was marrying Mr. Lockhart for his money, and it shamed her. But she would not submit herself to a conversation with the earl if his motive was to reproach her. "If you will excuse me—"

"No, please, wait." He followed her across the room, and she paused at the door. Rubbing the back of his neck, he wore a pained expression. "That was rude and unforgivable. I was thinking of the book, and I should never have likened it to your situation."

She narrowed her eyes, her heart thumping. "What do you know of my situation?"

"Nothing, which is precisely why I was asking." He clenched his jaw, the muscle moving back and forth as he glanced away and then set his gaze back on her. "But I had no right."

She pursed her lips, her chest rising and falling rapidly in time with her pounding pulse. "I may not have the luxury of choice, which I do not expect someone in your situation to understand. But what I do expect from you is the decency to allow that I know my own mind, and whatever decision I have made, it was consciously and carefully done."

"I wouldn't expect anything less from you, Miss Hatcher. I am ashamed of myself, and I hope you will forgive—as well as *forget*—how I've erred."

She nodded, but her heart continued to beat rapidly; she needed to get away from the earl, have a moment to collect herself before she faced Mr. Lockhart, her mother, and the rest of the Bright family. Stepping from the room, she slipped around the corner and into the antechamber—where the family gathered before mealtimes when there were no guests present—and leaned against the wall.

The hard, unfortunate truth to Lord Sanders's words bit at her heels like an unrelenting, yappy dog. She *had* chosen the comfort of a wealthy match because of the money it would provide and the peace she hoped would accompany it. But that was not the full truth, and the earl did not know the extent of her motivation. While the comfort of a fortune was beguiling, Mary had not agreed to marry Mr. Lockhart for his money alone.

She had done it for her mother's comfort. *That* was marrying for love, too.

CHAPTER 14

*M*ary perched on the edge of the sofa cushion in the drawing room following dinner, arranging her face into a picture of polite interest as she watched her betrothed converse with her hosts. Mr. Lockhart had a pleasant smile and an even disposition. He'd sat through dinner at Sanders House politely answering Lady Anne's multitude of questions with equanimity and poise and had endeared himself to Mama with compliments and smiles.

He was every bit as charming as she remembered, and the charisma he portrayed was not lost on any member of their party—not even the earl. Still, the longer the evening wore on, the less often Mary was able to meet Lord Sanders's gaze. Mr. Lockhart dripped money, from his fob-filled watch chain that jingled when he walked, to his ridiculously jeweled cravat pin.

Lord Sanders's earlier statement, when he had assumed she chose to marry someone she did not love, sat on her shoulders like an unwelcome feline. She could do nothing to defend her position without revealing the depth of her father's degradation—something that was far from within her power to divulge.

"My dear Miss Hatcher has had to put up with horrible scrawl these past few years."

Mr. Lockhart's words pulled Mary from her reverie, and she pasted a smile on her face, preparing to refute the claim when Lord Sanders spoke. "What does the handwriting matter when the letter is so eagerly anticipated?"

Mary swallowed her initial rebuttal, meeting the earl's gaze. Never mind that she only received two letters from Mr. Lockhart while he was away—and one of them a short missive detailing his return and naming their wedding date. "Of course. Who cares for the handwriting at all? It is the content of the letter that bears meaning, not its packaging."

"Is everything prepared for the wedding?" Lady Sanders asked, arranging her hands on her lap, seated on her usual settee. The remainder of the party was sitting on the settee and sofa around her, all present except for Lady Caroline, who had opted to eat upstairs and remain with her governess for the evening. Mary had invited her to join them, but Caroline had insisted she would be more comfortable upstairs. She was still young enough to believe most dining room conversations with anyone but her immediate family were naught but a bore.

"Indeed," Mr. Lockhart said. "Once we can make the trip home, the rest will be quite easily managed."

"And you have your trousseau now!" Lady Anne said, grinning. Her excitement was nearly palpable and not at all befitting the demure lady Society demanded her to be. But it was refreshing—Mary only hoped her betrothed would say nothing to diminish Lady Anne's spirit.

"Do you?" Mr. Lockhart asked, turning his attention on Mary.

She nodded, suddenly far more anxious than she probably ought to be. But why did he look so surprised? He *wanted* her to prepare a trousseau, did he not? "It was for that purpose that we traveled to London."

He watched her as if she had said the most interesting thing, his gaze tripping over her face, up to her hair, and then back down, traveling over the contours of her gown. Had he just considered the state of her dress? Her mouth grew dry, and she felt the need to cover herself, to hide her worn hem and pull from her hair the aged and ratty ribbon.

If only Father were here, he could step in and say something to distract Mr. Lockhart from Mary's dishevelment. She had tried so hard to make herself presentable, but it was an impossible feat when faced with four-year-old dresses and ribbons. Her earrings, while nice, were not what she'd been used to wearing when she was in the height of her social activity, and Mr. Lockhart's frank perusal probably hadn't missed a single thing.

Lord Sanders leaned back in his seat, casually resting an arm over the back of the sofa where his sister sat. "Did you say you were from Berkshire, Mr. Lockhart?"

"No, actually, I did not." Mr. Lockhart shot Mary a smile before eagerly settling his attention on the earl. Mary had not missed the way her betrothed had kept an eye on Lord Sanders all evening, as if he wanted to speak to the man but was waiting to be spoken to first. She had sensed his eagerness when she had introduced them at Gunter's as well; she could only assume he was already anxious to begin his social climb.

The very point that it was part of her wedding contract that she must give Mr. Lockhart a proper introduction to the *ton*, to procure an invitation to the Brights' summer house party, still felt odd to Mary. Though she tried to understand Mr. Lockhart's motives—*many* men of title and worth would be there and it would be an excellent opportunity for a man who did not grow up among the *ton* to make an entry into their world—there was a certain lack of sincerity in Mr. Lockhart's manner. It felt less about the *people* he interacted with and more about what he believed they could offer him.

But the Brights were not simpletons. They would see right through him.

Mary couldn't help but feel as though it would be easier to accomplish her task without Mr. Lockhart present. She imagined him eagerly awaiting news of a house party invitation, and it only increased the pressure she felt. He clearly wanted to be accepted by these people of high rank and esteem, but that was something he must earn on his own merit. A single party invitation was no promise. As it was, his own excessive eagerness would likely only hinder, not help his efforts.

"Mr. Lockhart became our neighbor only three years ago," Mama said, smiling kindly at the man. As far as she was aware, Mary's engagement was equally sought after and anticipated by both parties. And Mary did not wish for Mama to learn otherwise.

Mr. Lockhart sat on a chair between the sofas, settling his happy smile on Mary. "Taking the estate that bordered the Hatchers was one of the most fortuitous choices I have yet made. It led me to find this lovely woman."

Mary's cheeks flamed.

"Undoubtedly blessed, of course," Lord Sanders said, his words plain and clipped. "What took you to Berkshire? I was told you are in shipping."

"Out of Portsmouth, yes," he said, sitting taller in his chair. "But my mother was tired of the bustling town and longed to settle in the country, so I set my man to finding a worthy estate. I did not have any care for where we lived. I don't spend a good deal of time there anyway, so it was left to my mother to choose a house."

"And your father?"

"He has been gone from this world for quite some time."

Lord Sanders nodded, understanding. He turned to his sister, who had not ceased smiling since the moment Mr. Lockhart stepped foot in Sanders House. "Do you have the cards in here, Anne? We ought to ask Mr. Lockhart if he would like to play a round of whist."

"No, but I can easily ask Finch to fetch them."

"Does that interest you?" Lord Sanders asked, lifting his gaze to their guest.

Mr. Lockhart nodded. "I don't often indulge in cards, but I can make an exception this evening."

"Are you morally opposed?" Lady Anne asked.

"Not in the least. I am simply too busy most of the time."

Mary took that bit of information and stored it away for later, along with his admission that he was often too busy to be in Berkshire. She'd hoped this would be the case and was gratified by his confirmation. She appeared to be destined for a life at his estate with his mother while he traveled about England to maintain his business. She was not opposed to the idea, but the more she considered it, the more it occurred to her that she was entirely unaware of Mr. Lockhart's expectations for their marriage.

"Shall we play whist?" Lady Anne asked, rising from her seat on the sofa. The men stood and Mary followed them.

"Mother," Lord Sanders asked, "would you like to play?"

"No thank you, dear." She glanced at Mama on the sofa beside her. "I think we are quite comfortable here."

Mama smiled warmly, nodding at her friend, and Mary turned away to join the others at the card table.

Whenever they entertained at home, it was often Mary who sat stalwart by her mama's side all evening, ensuring she was comfortable, making sure she was not left alone, exposed to the possibility of conversation with anyone she didn't know well. Mama's shyness and discomfort knew no bounds. It had been something of a relieving break that Lady Sanders had seemed to step into that role since they had all come to London together. And not just so Mary might enjoy a break from playing the dutiful daughter—she loved her mother dearly and attending her was not a trial—but it was comforting that Lady Sanders appeared to enjoy the role and that her mother had relaxed so in her friend's presence.

Finch procured a stack of cards, and Lord Sanders set about shuffling and sorting them. He'd sat across from his sister, allowing Mary to partner with Mr. Lockhart.

"Do you plan to stay in London until Twelfth Night?" Lady Anne asked. She was all but bouncing in her seat, her gaze darting between Mary and Mr. Lockhart.

"I did not intend to, no." Mr. Lockhart's gaze slid to Mary. "But my plans can easily change."

"Oh, you most certainly should remain! There is a ball—"

"Lady Anne," Mary said quickly, her cheeks infusing with warmth. "It is not our place to make invitations to another person's ball."

Lady Anne glanced at her brother, her expression stricken, her mouth hanging open. "Oh, dear."

"Do not trouble yourself—" Mr. Lockhart began, but he was soon cut off.

Lord Sanders glanced up. "I am certain Lady Rutledge would not have any trouble with our bringing a guest. If it is agreeable to Mr. Lockhart, there is no reason you cannot extend the invitation, Anne."

Relief poured over her face. She swallowed, nodding.

Mr. Lockhart's deep voice remained steady. "That would be exceptionally kind of you, but I do not wish to intrude where I am not invited."

"But you were invited," Lord Sanders said. If it wasn't for the smile on his lips, Mary would have thought she heard an edge to his tone. Irritation, perhaps? "My sister just extended the invitation, and we would be happy to include you in our party. Lady Rutledge is an old friend of my mother's, and I am certain it will not be the least trouble. I will write to her myself on the matter."

"In that case, I would be absolutely delighted to join you."

Mary did her best to be grateful for the exchange that led to his addition to the Twelfth Night ball, but her stomach wound in knots anyway; she could not understand why the thought of him attending made her queasy. "That is wonderful, Mr. Lockhart."

Sitting across the table from her, his gaze settled on her face, unwavering. "In the meantime, Miss Hatcher, I was hoping we might manage to spend some time together. It is an unforeseen blessing, being quite stuck in London, is it not?"

She picked up her cards, putting them in the proper order to give her trembling fingers something to busy themselves with. "I believe it is, Mr. Lockhart."

He delivered a satisfied smile before arranging his own cards. All through the game of whist, and the subsequent two rounds, Mr. Lockhart casually inquired about the Bright family. He returned Lady Anne's inquisition from dinner with an even more thorough investigation. He was curious about Lord Sanders's schooling, the clubs he attended in Town, and whether there was much going on this time of year in the way of sport. Then he moved on to question Lady Anne about Lady Rutledge's ball and what he might expect there—specifically who he might see.

By the time the third game drew to a close, Mary was stunned silent. She'd hardly said two words throughout the duration of the games while Mr. Lockhart expertly maneuvered Lady Anne and Lord Sanders around his intellectual finger, learning what he could about the *ton* and their place in it.

If it was not clear to either of her hosts that Mr. Lockhart was an upstart who fully intended to climb the social hierarchy as far as he could, then they surely *were* simpletons. And Mary knew the Bright children were anything but simple. Lady Anne might have the fresh naivety befitting her age and position, but her brother was seasoned and intelligent.

More than once, Mary had felt the temptation to request a private word with Mr. Lockhart merely to ask him to cease his questioning. He may believe himself to be gathering information, but this sort of careless ignorance would not endear him to either of the Brights.

And above all, this was certainly not how one found themselves invited to a summer house party, from where he could make all the introductions he wished. Mary might not have been on familiar terms with Lord or Lady Sanders before now, but she had moved about the elite circles her entire life, and that had taught her how to behave. It appeared that Mr. Lockhart needed a lesson in what was expected from London's elite.

The hour drew late, and Mr. Lockhart pulled on his golden watch chain, flipping it open and then shutting it with a snap. "I must be off."

Lord Sanders rose, and Mary and Lady Anne followed suit. Mr. Lockhart crossed the room to thank his hostess and bid farewell to the mothers, then paused before the door, watching Mary.

Though his lips remained closed, his eyes spoke to her, intense excitement nearly palpating from them. As she hardly knew the man, it was hard to decipher what he was trying to tell her, but his gaze remained on her; she could only assume he was requesting that she come to his side. Crossing the room, Mary kept her hands clasped before her, only giving one to Mr. Lockhart when he reached for it.

"I would have hoped to be able to request your company for a ride in the park, but alas, it is too cold for any such jaunts."

"It is no matter, Mr. Lockhart. We shall have plenty of time for that when the snow melts."

"Then perhaps you will honor me with your company at dinner tomorrow. The Clarendon has a wonderful French chef, and I can attest to its exquisite fare." He glanced up, looking at the mothers. "In fact, I would be honored to have all of you to dine tomorrow night."

Every ear in the room had clearly turned to listen, and they needed no further clarification. Mary could feel the weight of Lady Anne watching them with poorly concealed anticipation, her brother blandly staring from behind her.

Lady Sanders gave a matronly smile. "That would be marvelous, Mr. Lockhart, if you are certain it would be no trouble."

He flashed a wide grin. "It will be no trouble at all. I shall plan to accept your party at eight."

Squeezing Mary's fingers, he brought her knuckles up to his lips and placed a kiss over them before dropping her hand and fleeing the room. Finch waited in the hall to show him out.

Mary stood, rooted to the hardwood floorboard, unable to move, and watched the space in the doorway where Mr. Lockhart had disappeared from.

Movement behind her gathered her attention and she turned, finding Lord Sanders standing directly behind her. He held out a book and she accepted it, surprised to find the third volume of *Pride & Prejudice*.

"You left it in here before dinner," he said, his blue gaze fixed on her, his brow serious. "I assumed you would want to continue reading now."

A smile curled her lips, and she pulled the book close to her chest, suddenly unconcerned with the multitude of worries that had assaulted her for the duration of Mr. Lockhart's visit. She breathed out, able to relax again. Lord Sanders and his family neither cared nor noticed her worn gown and old ribbon. They were simply pleased she was there.

Following the earl back to the sofas near the fire, Mary took a seat beside Lady Anne and opened the book to the place she had last read, tilting it toward the light. Things would settle down once they were married, of course. But then why had she felt such a cool wash of relief when Mr. Lockhart had left their party?

CHAPTER 15

*M*ary turned another page in her novel, leaning further toward the edge of the couch to catch the light from the waning fire. Both of the mothers had long since retired for the evening, and she was prepared to join the women soon in their quest for slumber, but she only had a few pages left in the book. Sleep could wait just a little longer.

The sharp scent of the evergreen boughs on the mantel was dulling along with the drying needles, but it wafted under her nose, bringing warmth and comfort to her heart. A soft, high snore came from the other end of the sofa and Mary pulled her gaze from the page, a smile on her lips as she looked to Lady Anne, leaning against the end of the sofa with a blanket over her legs, oblivious in her sleep to her mouth hanging agape.

Mary glanced at Lord Sanders seated on the sofa opposite them, his eyes settled lovingly on his sister. When he spoke, his voice was low, quiet. "She nearly didn't know how to properly act around Mr. Lockhart this evening, did she?"

"You are referring to her over-eagerness? I think it was sweet."

"She was *very* eager." A smile flickered over his lips. "Though who could blame her? She wanted to know your betrothed better. I believe we all did."

"I can't imagine why."

He tilted his head to the side, his eyes crinkling in bemusement. "You've quite endeared yourself to us, Miss Hatcher. Have you not seen that?"

Mary dropped her gaze, her neck heating. Lady Anne and Lady Caroline were sweet, and more than once she'd caught herself likening them to the sisters she wished she'd been blessed with. "I do adore your sisters."

"It is mutual."

Mary returned her attention to her book, flipping the final page and enjoying each happily situated word. When she finished the book, she closed it reverently and set it on her lap. Glancing up, she raised her eyebrows. "Go ahead, Lord Sanders. Enjoy your triumph."

"You enjoyed the story?"

"Very much."

He watched her, his smile warm. "And what do you make of the ending?"

She set the book on the small space of empty cushion between Lady Anne and herself and pulled her feet onto the sofa, tucking them underneath her. A yawn stole her poise, and she blushed. "It is far too late to discuss it in depth, but I quite liked it."

He mocked affront. "There is never a bad time to discuss books. And it is best to do so when the story is fresh, is it not?"

She conceded his point, unable to draw her attention from his glittering eyes, which reflected the dim firelight from the grate between them. "What do you make of Mr. Darcy?"

"He is proud, but then again, so is Miss Elizabeth."

"And his other faults?" she asked.

Lord Sanders smiled, his teeth gleaming. "He had many, did he not? But so did Miss Eliza. And yet, they both learned from their faults. Only consider where he began, how he fancied himself in love with her, begged her to marry him, and was shocked by her refusal."

"It was conceited of him to believe she could love him at that point, of course."

Lord Sanders paused, his voice low—likely so he did not wake his sister. "Yes, he had done much to earn her wrath. But after she went to his estate and witnessed the grandeur of Pemberley, which she could one day become mistress of, what did she do to show Mr. Darcy that she loved him for more than his house?"

Mary considered the question but quickly shifted to considering the man who asked it. Was he concerned that he would be in Mr. Darcy's position one day? That he would not be able to discern whether a woman loved him or his money? His title? His estates and prestige?

She plucked at the green overlay on her gown, pulling on a loose ivory embroidery thread. "I can only imagine that Mr. Darcy loved her enough to trust her. He loved her for her character, did he not? For the woman he believed her to be. If he could feel that way, then it stands to reason that he would know her well enough to know she would not say things she did not mean."

His eyebrows drew together in consideration, but she was not finished.

"And I do think she proved herself," Mary continued, "by refusing the initial proposal. She knew of his wealth at that time. If that was all she desired, she would have accepted him initially."

Lord Sanders stretched out his legs, crossing them at the ankles. He intertwined his fingers and rested them over his stomach. "That is a valid point, and one I had not considered." He regarded her closely. "Were you pleased that Miss Jane Bennet received her own satisfactory ending? I recall hearing you say that you were interested in her outcome."

"Yes. She deserved to be happy, and I was immensely satisfied with the ending."

He looked as though he wished to say more, but he remained silent.

Mary thought on the argument they'd had before dinner, and she turned her attention to the fire. They really ought to add a log, or it would burn out soon. The strong desire overcame her to apologize for Mr. Lockhart's behavior following dinner, but there was no way to do so without disrespecting the man she was going to marry, and she could not do such a thing. It would be wrong of her, disloyal.

"What are you thinking about so intently?" Lord Sanders asked, his voice husky.

"Mr. Lockhart."

The room grew silent but for the ticking clock, as if everything else had frozen. Lord Sanders cleared his throat. "He is very tall," he said. "And possessed of good manners."

She glanced at the earl. "Does that shock you? He is in trade, after all."

His head drew back, resting on the back of the sofa. "You cannot think I care whether he is in trade or not. I was merely making an observation."

She could not discern whether the earl was being polite or honest. She'd been so worried about Mr. Lockhart's inquisition, his boldness. "I confess I hardly know Mr. Lockhart, but he is a gentleman, and I am certain we will find our own rhythm eventually."

"If you hardly know him—"

"My father contracted the marriage." The silence in the room was so thick, Mary thought she could slice it with a knife. Lady Anne stirred on the sofa beside her, and she waited for the girl to rise, but she remained asleep. The dimness of the room and the quiet house had lulled Mary into a sense of being alone with Lord Sanders, and she found she had the strongest desire to confess the nature of her marriage contract to the earl.

The only people in the whole of England who were aware of the circumstances were her father, her betrothed, and herself. Would it be so very terrible to confide in another? In someone she deemed a friend? She swallowed the impulse. It was juvenile and silly. She had lived many years without someone to confide in, and she could easily continue in the same manner.

But it did strike her as funny how similar Mr. Lockhart's faults were to the fictional Mr. Darcy.

"What are you thinking about?" Lord Sanders asked. "Your eyebrows have been dancing together and apart, and it is quite concerning."

Mary laughed quietly. "I was thinking of my marriage contract with Mr. Lockhart. And how very similar he is to Mr. Darcy."

"Oh. How so? Does he own half of Derbyshire?"

She smiled. "No, but he has a lot of pride in his accomplishments, and I do not fault him for it. He thinks in terms of business in a way I could never quite wrap my brain around."

"You claim not to know him well, and then you speak as though the opposite is true."

She stilled, startled by his blunt honesty. "I don't know him very well at all. But my little acquaintance has taught me much. Our marriage is a business arrangement. That speaks quite a lot about the both of us, does it not?"

"It explains why you were so quick to defend Charlotte Lucas's choice to marry Mr. Collins earlier tonight."

So, he had not forgotten their argument. Mary wanted to duck her head, to hide her embarrassment, but she held the earl's gaze. "Sometimes we are able to make our own choices, and sometimes we do things simply because we must."

He uncrossed his ankles and leaned forward, resting his elbows on his knees. "Do you not wish to..." He paused, clearing his throat, his eyes dark and solemn. "That is, I mean to ask if you are certain..."

He seemed unable to finish a coherent thought, but she thought she knew what he was trying to ask. "I am content with my choice. I've had quite a lot of time to settle my heart on the matter. But it matters not what I think; the contract has been signed, the agreement already made."

"Contracts have been broken before."

Her heart leapt in her chest, pounding furiously, before she tamped it down, pouring reality over it like a bucket of water over a fire. "It is impossible. And I ought to go to sleep." She stood, crossing her arms over her chest. "Can I trust you to wake your sister, or should I do so now?"

"Wait," he begged, standing. "I cannot rest with this laying on my conscience. Have you been coerced into making this agreement?"

She wanted so badly to confide in him, but what would it mean? How could she burden him with her troubles? If nothing else, she ought to put him at ease. "I will only answer your question if you answer one of mine."

"Deal," he said without hesitation, the quick-thinking of a man used to wagers.

She lifted her chin, meeting his eyes. "Mr. Lockhart has purchased my father's debts. He pulled us from the mires of destitution and restored my father's good name. And he only did these things as part of our marriage contract. If I was to step away, to break our engagement, my father would be forced to repay Mr. Lockhart, and that is impossible."

Lord Sanders leaned back, his widened eyes stricken. "So the man bought you?"

Cool distaste prickled her skin and slithered down her spine. She had *felt* like a commodity when her father and Mr. Lockhart set about preparing the agreement, but they had been careful to treat her with dignity and respect—to give every appearance of allowing Mary a choice, even though she knew she lacked one. "I am doing my part to save my family's name. And I would appreciate it if you put this information from your mind. You are one of four people now in possession of this knowledge, and I would prefer my mother never learned of it."

His eyes hardened. "You cannot mean you've led your mother to believe you developed a *tendre* for Mr. Lockhart?"

Andrew was doing his level best to keep his voice even, his breathing controlled, but the information Mary had just given him was the outside of enough. Her father had *sold* her to that upstart, Lockhart? If only Andrew had known her before, he could have easily pulled her father from the depths of his debt and done so without bartering for a wife.

He knew it was a common practice, especially among those of old titles who wished to replenish their wealth, but to know *Mary's* happiness hung in the balance of such a crude agreement made him ill.

"My mother knows we came to an agreement after very little acquaintance. What she makes of that is up to her, but she has been kept fully unaware of the depth of my father's losses. I believe she thinks that if we retrench long enough, we will come about all right again, that our economizing is temporary. And she is not wrong."

"Are these losses from gambling?"

"Speculation," she corrected.

"Ah," Andrew said, nodding. "A gentleman's folly. It is a gamble, but a much more calculated one."

She narrowed her eyes. "You do not approve of speculation?"

"My father did not. He'd known too many good men lose fortunes to see any value in it. He warned me away at length, and I've never forgotten."

"I would have liked to have had the opportunity to meet your father."

Andrew's chest warmed. "He would have liked you."

"You cannot know that, but it is kind of you to say, nonetheless." She shifted, her eyes growing serious. "But I answered your question, so now it is my turn to ask one."

He met her gaze. What could she possibly wish to know about him? "Yes?"

"What is your favorite Christmas memory?"

He was not expecting that question. Looking down into her curious eyes, he swallowed his apprehension. "My favorite memory involved my father, actually."

She remained standing, her hands clasped in front of her, intently listening to him speak.

"When I was no more than ten years old, my father came to me late one afternoon just after Christmas and quietly asked me to prepare to go for a ride on our sled. It was to be a surprise, and I could not let anyone know what I was up to. So I dressed in all of my winter clothes, snuck out of the house, and met him at the stables. He'd harnessed his horse to the sled and he helped me in, covering me with a blanket."

Anne shifted on the sofa and Andrew glanced at her, watching to see if she was waking. Gratefully, she seemed to stay asleep; he was not yet ready to end his conversation with Mary. He gestured to the vacant sofa behind them, and Mary nodded before she took a seat at the end nearest the fire, and he followed her over. He made sure to leave enough distance between them to be respectful, but sit close enough that he could speak softly, and she would hear him.

"That sounds like a fun experience for a young boy."

"It gets better," he said, unable to temper his smile. The fond memories of that night still soothed his grieving heart whenever he missed his father. "We usually had bells attached to the sled, but they had been removed that night, and when I asked why, my father explained that we were acting in secret and needed to do our utmost to not get caught."

Mary's eyebrows rose, her interest piqued, he hoped.

"We rode to the vicarage in the center of town where the vicar's wife had recently given birth to a baby boy, and my father pulled to a stop away from the building, down the street. He handed me a small box and told me to put it on the doorstep, knock on the door, and run back to the sled as quickly as I was able without being seen."

"What was in the box?"

"He never told me exactly what it contained. It was just a little something to help them out; that was all the explanation I received. We went on to deliver a dozen other boxes that evening before we went home and put the sled and horse away and snuck back into the house. I pestered him for more information, but he only told me that we had done the work of the angels that night, and I was never to reveal our actions to another soul. He explained that he enjoyed serving God's children most when others weren't watching. That he felt it was special, just between him and God and the person he served."

"Did you not wish to know what was in the boxes?"

"Of course I did," he said, chuckling. He recalled his earnest curiosity as a young boy, but the way his father had explained the situation resonated with him, even at so tender an age. It meant a lot to Father, so he had let it go. "All he would tell me was that he knew they had each had a need, and we had filled part of that need."

Mary's voice was quiet, filled with awe. "And you never told anyone?"

He smiled, remembering his solemn promise as a young boy, and how desperately important he thought it was to keep the secret. He had felt so special sharing that with his father. "No, I never told anyone."

"Until now."

"Yes."

She smiled guiltily. "You needn't have told me."

"You asked for my favorite Christmas memory. I wanted to be honest."

Mary reached over and placed her hand on Andrew's, and he went still. Squeezing his fingers, she gazed at him with compassion. "Your father sounds like a good man. It is no wonder you serve your sisters so well. You clearly had an excellent example."

"Thank you," he said, and he wondered if she heard his words, so difficult it was to choke them out. He cleared his throat. "I know I will never measure up to him, and neither do I try."

"You may not see it, but I imagine you are very much like him."

He wanted to slip his hand from hers, to put space between them and end this uncomfortable conversation, but he did not wish to lose the contact of her fingers on his. They had both shed their gloves earlier in the night and her soft skin was warm, comforting him.

Her eyebrows pulled together, her eyes resting on him in earnest interest. "Why is it that you don't believe you measure up?"

He lifted his shoulder in a soft shrug. "It is nothing. I just know how good he was, and how I lack. I am not a paragon. I do not serve others selflessly, climb upon roofs to fix thatches, deliver secret packages to my neighbors in need. I gamble, wager, drink, and play cards. I am more concerned with my own entertainment than I am suffering through a winter in the country with my mother."

"You have told me all of this before, but I still cannot believe it sinks you as low as you believe it does. What will it take for you to understand that you are likely exactly the man your father wanted you to be? You care for your sisters and your mother. You serve others by remembering their preference for oranges and evergreen boughs and go out of your way to procure them. You play games you'd rather not simply because your sisters wish it." She squeezed his fingers again, and he felt it clear in his heart. "In what way have I described a man who is only after his own gain?"

"Yes, that all *sounds* good, but—" He scrubbed a hand over his face, unsure how to explain this to her. He was not inherently good like his father. "I do not put others above myself."

"I only just gave you examples of how you do exactly that."

She was difficult to persuade. "Yes, but I have done none of those things without grumbling about the snow or the cold or about being forced to celebrate a holiday I'd much rather pass playing cards with my friends in our clubs."

"But you didn't, Andrew. You chose to remain here with your family, to suffer the cold to find your sister some evergreen, to participate in a childish puppet show to bring a smile to Caroline's, Anne's, and your mother's faces. Accept what I am telling you: you are more like your father than you think."

The room grew dimmer as the fire waned more, and what little flame remained jumped about, dancing light across Mary and Andrew. Their clasped hands glowed orange, and he hoped she would remain in that position forever. Had she realized that she'd called him Andrew? It had felt so natural and sounded charming on her lips.

"I understand the points you are trying to make, and I appreciate you for trying to make them."

But she did not know his father.

Mary slipped her hand from his, taking all the warmth left in the room with it. He longed to reclaim her hand, to sit like that all night and ask her to share stories of her childhood as well. But he did not have a claim on Mary.

She yawned, bringing her hand up to cover her mouth, and then stood. "Shall I wake Lady Anne and take her upstairs with me?"

"I will see to her. You may go on ahead."

Mary gave him a grateful, pointed smile as if to say, *See? I told you so.*

He wanted to argue that this was his duty as a brother and a gentleman and nothing more, but he had a feeling that would lead to a fruitless argument. Mary would not be swayed.

"Goodnight, my lord."

"Goodnight."

He watched her walk away, leaning back on the sofa and considering her words. Could they hold an ounce of truth? Certainly he would never be so selfless and humble as the late earl had been. But perhaps his small efforts were making a difference in the lives of his family. He could not replace Father, but he could ease the pain of his absence.

Anne's voice cut through the quiet room and startled Andrew. "I really like Mary."

"Gads, Anne! You could warn a man first."

She straightened on the sofa opposite him, rubbing at her tired eyes.

Unease crept upon him, and he looked at her warily. "How long have you been awake?"

"Long enough to hear you tell her of your secret outing with Father."

So she had been awake when Mary had taken his hand, too. His cheeks warmed, and he was grateful the darkness in the room likely hid his blush from his sister. He could only hope that her pretending to sleep had hidden their hands from her as well.

But even if they hadn't, things would still be well. Neither he nor Mary had done anything wrong.

"You do realize that Father did the same thing with me, right?"

Andrew paused, narrowing his eyes at his sister. "What do you mean? The Christmas deliveries?"

"Yes." She stretched her arms high above her head. "And I never told a soul because he begged me to keep it a secret. But I was quite young, and likely not as fast as you were, because I was caught."

"By a tenant?"

She shook her head. "By Mrs. Phillips. The woman who lived down by the bridge? I slipped on the ice when I was running away, and she must have been near her door when I knocked because she was outside at once, helping me to my feet and offering to bring me inside to warm near the fire. I went with her, and father had to come in and fetch me; by the time he followed me inside, she had opened the box."

"What was in it?"

"Gloves, shoes for the Phillips children, and a sack of coins. It had been a heavy box compared to the others, and I'm certain Father gave her a good deal of money."

Money? Shoes? Andrew's young imagination had created a vision of carved, wooden soldiers and geography puzzles much like he'd wished for as a child, not items of necessity. It quite made sense though. What would the vicar's wife have done with toy soldiers?

He rubbed his jaw. "When was this?"

"It was the winter after her husband died and left her a widow. Father told me she needed extra help and made me promise never to tell a soul. He told me my blessings would be greater if I kept the secret because it was just between us, Mrs. Phillips, and God."

Andrew nodded, remembering having that similar conversation with his father. "He was a good man."

"As are you."

Andrew rose, ignoring the comment. So Anne had heard all of that part, too. He was unprepared to have this conversation with a member of his family.

"I heard what Mary told you, Andrew, and I agree with her. You are too hard on yourself."

"I could do better."

Anne scoffed, rising from the sofa and taking his arm. "Oh, pish. Of course you could. Is there a person alive who couldn't do better?"

She let him lead her upstairs in silence, seemingly respecting that most of the house was already asleep, and didn't say another word on the matter.

That night Andrew lay in bed watching the moonlight glow against his open window and wondering if there was any truth to Mary's or Anne's words.

CHAPTER 16

"*D*o you think Mr. Lockhart will be upset that we've arrived early?" Lady Anne asked, pressing into Mary's side on the plush bench seat so she might look out the small window. Their shoulders bumped as the carriage rolled to a stop outside of the tall, brick building, the black letters displayed across the sign depicting the hotel's name.

Lord Sanders shook his head. "Of course he will not be angry. We are only a quarter-hour early, and he would not expect us to wait in the carriage in this cold, Anne."

Mary hoped that would be the case. Mr. Lockhart was so eager to please the Brights, she rather thought the earl was correct. They could likely do no wrong where he was concerned.

The door swung open, and a servant let down the step. Lord Sanders stepped out before turning around to help the women down onto the snow-covered ground. Lady Anne and her mother removed first, and Lord Sanders reached for Mrs. Hatcher's hand. "Be cautious, madam. The road is slick."

Mary scooted to the end of the bench, taking the earl's gloved fingers and stepping into the bitter cold. The sky was dark, the group's breath clouding before them as they waited for the entirety of their party to exit the carriage. Lights from the street lamps cast a weak orange glow over the walkway in both directions, highlighting the misty air.

"Oh, Mary!" Lady Anne hissed, reaching for her as she stepped closer to the building. Her blonde ringlets were hidden under a wide bonnet, but the evening shadows did not hide her stricken face, white as if she'd seen a ghost.

Mary jumped, startled by the harshness of her friend's tone. "What is it?"

Lady Anne hurried closer, looking over her shoulder as she did, and slipped. Her feet rammed into Mary's ankle as she pitched backward, her eyes widening until her head hit the brick step that led up to the hotel.

"Anne!" Mary screamed, dropping to her knees and lifting Lady Anne's head from the cold ground onto her lap.

Lord Sanders was next to her on the ground immediately. "Anne," he repeated, but neither of their summons roused the girl. Her eyes were closed, her face eerily still.

Looking over his shoulder, Lord Sanders shouted to his coachman. "Hold the carriage."

"What is it?" a deep voice asked behind them, and Mr. Lockhart appeared.

"We must get Anne home immediately. She's fallen and hit her head." Lord Sanders paused on Mr. Lockhart's face. "Can you find a physician? Send him to Sanders House."

"I don't—that is, I'm not sure where—"

The earl did not waste time. He looked to Mary. "Tell my groom to find a doctor."

She looked down. "But Andrew, I can't set her on the ground."

"Give her here." His arm slid carefully under his sister's shoulders, hefting her from the frozen ground and into his arms. His mother stood behind him, watching the scenario unfold with a handkerchief to her tear-stained face, Mama beside her, clutching her arm.

Mary rose, crossing to the groom behind the carriage and relaying the earl's message. "You must get a physician immediately." The man nodded before turning to glance down the road, then taking off at a run.

"Mr. Lockhart," Mary said, stepping nearer to the hotel where her intended stood, shocked. "I am afraid we cannot consider dinner right now."

"No, of course not. You must see to Lady Anne." His concerned expression did him credit. "But allow me to help. Might I escort you home?"

"I really must go with Lady Anne."

"Then I shall see to your mother. If Lady Anne is lying on the seat, surely there is not enough room for your entire party inside the carriage."

Mary nodded. She stepped forward, finding Lord Sanders within, his sister laying across the bench, her torso in her brother's arms. They could likely all fit on the opposite bench, but it would be a squeeze. And Lady Sanders would wish to be with her children.

She hurried to her mother's side. "Mama, let us help Lady Sanders into the carriage. Mr. Lockhart has offered to see us home directly, but they must lose no time."

"Of course," Mama agreed. They helped Lady Sanders up into the carriage, and Lord Sanders caught her gaze before she closed the door, his eyes sunken, tormented. She stepped back, watching the coachman urge the horses on until the carriage swayed forward and around the bend.

"Now let me hail a hackney," Mr. Lockhart said, disintegrating the image of Lord Sanders's distress from her mind. "It will be much faster."

"Thank you, sir," Mama said, her shoulders shaking with cold. Mary slid her arm around her mother, rubbing her arm to warm her while they waited for Mr. Lockhart to get them a cab. She stared into the distance, watching where Mr. Lockhart disappeared to, her mouth pinched in a firm line.

"She'll be all right, Mama. She must be."

"Hmm?" Mama turned, kissing Mary on the temple. "Oh, yes. We must hurry back so we can help."

Mary's ankle began to throb, the force of Lady Anne's kick as she'd gone down on the ice beginning to take an effect. Or perhaps the agitation of the event was beginning to wane, and she could feel it more acutely. She longed to sit, to raise her ankle and give it a moment to rest.

"Do you know your Mr. Lockhart well, my dear?" Mother asked suddenly, her voice measured and soft.

"I know him as well as you do," Mary confessed. In fact, they both knew his mother better than they knew him. But even that was not much.

"Hmm." Mother said no more, and Mr. Lockhart returned, gesturing the women to the waiting hackney in the street. A strange expression fell over Mama's face as she thanked the man, and Mary climbed onto the worn seat, making room for her mother and her betrothed.

She could not remove from her mind the very strange expression on her mother's face and wondered precisely what it meant.

To Andrew's blessed relief, Anne had begun to rouse when he'd carried her up to her bedchamber. His heart had been hammering in his chest from the moment he'd watched Anne slip on the slushy ground and her eyes had closed, the dreadful stillness overtaking her face.

"She's waking," he called over his shoulder and heard his mother moan in relief.

They settled Anne on her bed, Mother murmuring comforting words to her as her maid set about removing her shoes and sliding woolen stockings over her feet.

Andrew paced the bedroom, unsure of how to be useful. He gripped his cravat and loosened the knot. "Where is the doctor?" he demanded.

"I am certain he will be here as soon as he is able," Mother soothed.

"That is not quick enough for my taste," Andrew grumbled, turning back to pace to the fireplace again. Footsteps echoed in the corridor but were much too light to be a gentleman's boots. Mary and her mother stepped into the room, glancing about until their sights rested on Anne, awake, but with her eyes squeezed shut.

"She is awake," Mary said, her voice so quiet he hardly registered her words.

Andrew approached her. "She woke when we arrived home. But she hasn't spoken yet."

Mary nodded. A figure appeared in the doorway behind her, and Andrew moved to meet the man, only to find Mr. Lockhart and not the doctor he anticipated. Running an agitated hand through his hair, Andrew shot a perfunctory smile at the man before turning back to pace to the window.

"Lady Anne?" Mr. Lockhart's deep voice penetrated the room, but he did not step inside. Indeed, he should remove himself from their house.

Mary's voice replied, but Andrew could not make out what she said. He could only feel gratitude when he turned to find the upstart gone and Mary moving toward Anne's bedside.

"Andrew, you are going to wear a hole directly through that floor if you do not cease your pacing," Mother said sharply.

He stilled, glancing up to find every eye in the room—including the maid's—settled on him. He was something of a nervous wreck, wasn't he? "Perhaps I will go downstairs and await the doc—"

"Good evening, Lord Sanders, Lady Sanders," Dr. Kent said, sweeping into the room, the butler, Finch, standing in the corridor directly behind him. "I was informed that Lady Anne took a fall."

He approached the bed and smiled at Anne, his kind eyes crinkling at the corners.

"Outside of the Clarendon Hotel," Mother said. "She hit her head on the steps."

"Ah. May I?"

Mother stepped back, and Mrs. Hatcher moved to her side, sliding an arm around her back and offering support. Mary hesitated at the edge of the room, watching. Andrew did not know whether to leave the doctor to his business or remain and watch. He was so anxious, his body felt as though it hummed, his feet unable to remain still. When the doctor leaned down and began asking questions of Anne, Andrew knew he needed to make his escape. She was in good, trustworthy hands, and Andrew was likely making things worse with his agitated concern, not better.

Letting himself into the hallway, he took the stairs rapidly up two flights before he could go no higher, and then he turned and sped all the way to the ground floor. Resting both hands against the wall, Andrew leaned forward, his chest heaving and his head hanging. His sister, young, sweet, delicate Anne had fallen and hit her head so hard on the step that Andrew had heard the impact. It rang through his mind repeatedly; he wanted to remove it entirely but he did not know how.

"Lord Sanders?"

He stilled, his arms flexing at the sound of Mary's voice.

"May I do anything to help?"

"Is Dr. Kent with Anne?" he asked.

"Yes. He is continuing his examination. Although..."

Andrew's head snapped up. "What is it?"

Mary's round eyes widened. She must think him fit for bedlam with his crazed concern. She swallowed, stepping forward and laying a calm hand on his bicep. He flexed again on impulse, but her hand remained. "The doctor has not shared his thoughts yet, but I can only believe that his tone of voice would not be so cheerful if he was vastly concerned for her welfare."

Her words, so softly spoken, were a balm to his spirit, draining the fear from his body as though her hand on his arm was, in actuality, a spigot, and she had emptied his reserves. She made a valid point, but it was her presence of mind as well as body that calmed him, aided him in returning to a reasonable man of sound mind. The overwhelming desire to feel her in his arms crushed him, stealing his breath.

"Would you like to return to Anne's room? Or shall I come and find you when the doctor has finished his examination?"

Right. Anne. Andrew was ashamed for the direction his thoughts had traveled. His sister was upstairs and needed—he gasped. His *sister*. "Has anyone spoken to Caroline?"

Mary's face reflected the surprise he felt. "Oh, dear Caroline. Shall I go up now, or would you wish to?"

He would make an absolute mash of things if it was left to him. But what would Caroline need? A woman's loving support, surely. He smiled, but he could feel how crooked it was. "I think it best if you go."

"You do not think she will need to seek comfort from her brother?"

"I am certain you will provide the comfort she needs."

Mary stared at him, her brows pulling together as small lines formed between them. "What if we go together?"

The idea surprised him, but he found himself nodding and, shortly after, following Mary up the many flights of stairs to Caroline and her governess's rooms. "Should you explain?" he asked, but Mary merely glanced at him while her knuckles rapped softly on the door.

Miss Bolton opened the door, her hair swept low into a conservative bun, her middle-aged eyes wan. "Yes, my lord? Miss Hatcher?"

"We would like to speak to Caroline. Has she completed her dinner?"

"Yes, miss, long since passed." The governess stepped away, opening the door wide enough to allow them entry. The room was set up like the parlor downstairs; on one side, a table, on the other, a large globe surrounded by shelves of books.

Caroline sat on a rose, tufted chair near the fire, a book in her hands. "Good evening, Andrew, Mary. You are home early."

Andrew's feet were glued to the floor, but Mary crossed the room, lowering herself onto the footstool before Caroline's chair and taking the book from her hands. She set it on the floor and possessed herself of both of Caroline's hands. "When we arrived at the hotel for dinner,

Anne slipped in the snow and fell. She is in her bed now, and the doctor is seeing to her, but she hit her head on the step."

Caroline's small mouth opened in a gasp, and she glanced up, looking to Andrew with concern shining in her blue eyes. "Will she be all right?"

"We have yet to hear. We wanted you to be aware of the situation."

"We must go to her at once," Caroline said, standing and dropping Mary's hands.

Mary rose beside her, slipping her hand behind Caroline's back. "We don't wish to bring excitement into her chamber, so if you need a moment to compose yourself it would be wise to do so here."

Caroline nodded, and she turned, wrapping her arms around Mary in the embrace Andrew wished to have. Mary returned the hug, and then Caroline took in a deep breath. She crossed the room to Andrew and slid her small arms around his waist, pulling him close as she breathed against his chest.

Surprise filled him, but he quickly shoved it aside and returned his sister's embrace. She stepped back, looking up at him, worried. "Will you come with me?"

She wanted him? Of course he would be there with her when she needed him. He'd felt so useless after laying Anne on her bed earlier, so unaware of what he could possibly do to be of assistance. But now Caroline needed him. And he would do whatever she asked.

"Of course."

She slipped her small hand around his arm, and he led her from the room, glancing over his shoulder to ensure Mary was following. She stepped behind them, her hands clasped lightly in front of her and a joyful, satisfied smile on her lips.

He knew just how she felt.

CHAPTER 17

*A*fter his initial examination, the doctor had nothing but good things to report: he believed Anne would sustain no lasting effects from the fall, he believed the worst she would endure would be a nasty headache, and—most importantly, according to the patient—he had full faith in her ability to sustain complete recovery by Twelfth Night.

Mary closed the door to Lady Anne's bedchamber softly behind her, leaving the girl asleep with her maid nearby in case she needed anything. It had been a full two days since the wretched fall, and the doctor had just been in to visit and check her progress. He was a young man with a kind smile, and Mary liked him.

She almost asked him to take a look at her ankle, too, but after a decent night's rest it had already begun to feel better; she could not have been seriously hurt then, merely bruised.

Trailing her fingers along the evergreen lining the bannister, she paused at the base of the stairs and leaned forward, inhaling the scent from the dried needles interspersed with holly. Deep voices trailed up the stairwell, and when she recognized the doctor's smooth tone, she moved forward at once. Pausing at the base of the stairs, she found the doctor and the earl deep in conversation, Lord Sanders's back to her.

"And you think she will be fit for dancing?" Lord Sanders inquired, his brow furrowed. "She has been quite looking forward to it."

"Head injuries are oftentimes unpredictable, and I can make no promises. But I believe Lady Anne will be fit for dancing. She likely needs one or two more days of rest to allow the headache time to pass, and then she will be back to her bright, chipper self." His gaze flicked to Mary, and he offered her a brief smile.

Lord Sanders nodded, running an agitated hand through his hair. "Thank you, Dr. Kent."

"Of course. But now, I must beg your leave. I am sure you heard of Mr. Bartlett's unfortunate collision? His coachman walked away unscathed, but that poor family is soon to be without a father if things continue to progress the same way."

"I had not heard. I am afraid I'm unacquainted with any Bartletts."

The doctor's eyes widened. "Mrs. Bartlett is a cousin to Lady Rutledge, so I assumed—"

"Oh, yes, of course. I was not thinking." Lord Sanders's hands came behind him, his gloveless fingers clasping lightly together.

"If you are a praying man, then I would ask you to include Mr. Bartlett in your prayers. If he is lost, his family will be left with no home."

Mary's chest tightened. A cool gust of air wound into the corridor as the door opened and Dr. Kent left the house. Lord Sanders turned, halting the moment his eyes landed on her. "Forgive me," she begged. "I hadn't meant to overhear. I was only coming downstairs."

He nodded. And surely the doctor had not shared anything she need not know—he'd seen her standing just a few steps behind them.

"It was nothing overly personal."

"That poor family," she said. "I will be sure to pray for Mr. Bartlett. I only met Lady Rutledge once, just last week, but I know she is a dear friend to your mother. I cannot imagine suffering such hardship during Christmas, for the holiday to be so tainted by grief and anxiety."

Lord Sanders stepped closer. "I wish there was something we could do for them, but I fear this is not a case where a box of charity will make much difference."

Mary stored that thought away for further consideration at a later time. "I was just about to go in search of Lady Caroline."

"Allow me to join you?"

"Certainly."

He fell into step beside her as Mary began down the corridor toward the library. The mothers were both in their chambers, enjoying the afternoon in the same way Lady Anne was—asleep. It made the house unusually quiet.

She chuckled. "I admit, I had assumed the two of you would already be together."

Lord Sanders sent her a wry smile. From the moment they went to Lady Caroline's room to inform her of her sister's fall a few evenings before, she had clung to her brother. Mary hadn't seen the two apart since.

"She left me to speak to the doctor in private."

"You know where to find her then?"

He lifted one guilty shoulder. "I assumed she would come find me again when I was finished."

They passed a decorative table in the hallway holding a round vase full of hothouse flowers, bright red roses unseen in the natural gardens that were now covered in a thick blanket of white snow. But the sight gave her pause, and she halted in her steps.

"Did Lady Anne not wish to have her flowers in her room?"

Lord Sanders shook his head, leaning one shoulder against the mustard-colored wall beside the drawing room door and crossing his arms over his chest. "It was the oddest thing, actually. When I showed Anne the card that accompanied the flowers she asked that they be removed from her room."

Mary reached for a stem, careful to avoid the thorns, and twisted the flower softly in her fingers. "But Mr. Lockhart sent these. Does she have an aversion to roses?"

"Not in the least. My mother told me they were her favorite. I passed that information on to Mr. Lockhart when he called yesterday to ask after Anne."

"Perhaps her tastes have changed."

Lord Sanders was quiet for a moment, watching Mary. She smelled the heady, floral rose and then straightened, dropping it back in the vase.

His mouth was firm, his jaw set. "Perhaps."

"Why do I have the impression that you don't believe that?" Mary asked. "What has Mr. Lockhart done to earn Lady Anne's contempt?"

"Nothing that I am aware of."

"You did not think to ask her?"

"I did not think it was my place to do so."

Mary could not endure the earl's stare any longer. She stepped around him to enter the drawing room but lit upon a thought and paused directly before the door, turning toward him. "If you or your sister were to learn something unsavory about my...about Mr. Lockhart, you would tell me so, right?"

He pivoted against the wall to face her, his blue eyes stormy, almost gray. "If you wish it."

"Why would I not wish it?"

"You spoke yourself of the benefits of looking at marriage as a business arrangement. I did not know how engaged your heart was in the matter nor how much you would care."

Her heart thumped wildly in her chest at the very mention of it. That Lord Sanders thought of her wishes or cares at all seemed to send a wild flutter through her body. She tried to stomp down her heightened nerves, to make her face plain and her voice steady. "I am still a woman, Lord Sanders, and I find that no matter how deeply I wish to smother my emotions, they have a way of crawling to the surface anyway. Whether I want it or not, my feelings are engaged in all matters."

"You speak as though you care—"

The door to the drawing room opened, and Lady Caroline stood there, framed by the light from the tall, open windows behind her and making her blonde curls glow. "Oh, good! I was only just coming to search for you, Andrew. But, look!" She pointed up, above the doorway.

Mary and Lord Sanders's gazes followed her direction, and Mary froze. Hanging above them was the kissing bough she had made days ago, the very one the earl had hung above the door for her.

"The kissing bough!" Lady Caroline clapped her hands together, her smile wide. "You know what this means, of course."

Lord Sanders looked to Mary, his gaze dropping to her lips. She could not help but do the same, to notice how soft and enticing his lips looked.

Her body went completely still as guilt and hope warred within her.

Lord Sanders cleared his throat and reached for her hand, lifting one eyebrow. "May I?"

May he *what* exactly? Mary could not allow him to actually kiss her, regardless of how much the idea thrilled her. She was being disloyal from that thought alone and wanted to turn and run from the house, to give herself enough solitude to sort her feelings and put them all where they belonged. She was supposed to want to kiss Mr. Lockhart, not the earl.

He lifted her hand; she did not resist when his fingers squeezed hers and he bent to place a kiss over her knuckles. Disappointment and relief swirled together in her stomach, and Mary forced a smile, reclaiming her hand as she turned to enter the drawing room.

She passed an absolutely radiant Lady Caroline and sat down on the settee near the fire in time to see Lord Sanders pick a berry from the kissing bough and pocket it.

"I have been waiting forever, Andrew. What has the doctor said?"

He stepped around his eager sister and claimed a seat on the sofa opposite Mary, on the farthest cushion possible. Was he regretting kissing her hand? He was certainly putting as much space between them now as he feasibly could. She rubbed a thumb over her gloves where his lips had pressed, the warmth seeping through and staining her skin.

"Dr. Kent has decided that Anne will make a full recovery within the next few days. She has had no lasting effects from the fall despite her headaches, and he expects them to wane with time."

Caroline came to sit beside Mary. "That is good news, yes?"

Lord Sanders nodded. "Very good. It could have been significantly worse."

"Then what shall we do now?"

"Wait," he said with a shrug. "Hope she is past the worst of the headaches before the ball. For her sake, of course. I would be more than happy to skip it entirely." He winked at his sister.

"Please do skip it. Then you could remain here with me."

"Your mother would probably be sad to lose her escort," Mary said.

Lady Caroline groaned. "I do not look forward to balls in the slightest, but I do look forward to the day when you cease to leave me behind during your fun endeavors."

"We do not always leave you behind," Lord Sanders argued. "Just a few days ago you came with us to Gunter's, did you not?"

"Yes. But what about the Royal Menagerie or Covent Garden or Hyde Park? I *know* Anne went to the Frost Fair, and she did not bring me then, either."

Mary's head snapped around. "How did you learn of that?"

"Anne told me."

"But I thought...she said it was meant to stay a secret. She was afraid of troubling your mother."

Lady Caroline looked at Mary as though she had spoken in Greek. "Well, of course I am not going to tell my mother. She would be very disturbed. She thinks it a place for lowborn people of no morals."

Mary's body filled with relief. "Well, it was not anything like that. But you mustn't repeat that I said so." She glanced up and caught Lord Sanders's smile, returning a hesitant one of her own.

It was, after all, where they had met. Or perhaps collided was more accurate.

"Well, what say you to an outing today?"

"The Frost Fair?"

Lord Sanders laughed, the low, deep voice penetrating Mary's nerves. "It's gone now, Caro. But even if it wasn't, I would not take you somewhere Mother expressly forbade."

"But Anne—"

"*I* did not take Anne," he retorted, sending Mary another pointed look.

In her defense, neither had she. She had merely gone along so her friend would not go on her own into a dangerous city.

"Then to Gunter's again? Or Hatchard's?"

"You'd like to go to the bookstore?" Lord Sanders asked. "I suppose that could be managed. If it is agreeable to Miss Hatcher?"

Mary nodded. She would never refuse an outing that involved books.

Lord Sanders stood. "Then let's be off."

It took just under a half-hour to dress for the frigid, winter outing. Lord Sanders instructed Finch to have the carriage brought around, and Mary knew she only had a few minutes before she needed to be down in the entryway ready to leave.

She snuck into Lady Anne's room with the intention of asking if she would like them to pick up a book for her. Creeping across the floor, she paused at the foot of the bed and peered down at the slumbering girl. Lady Anne looked so much younger with her hair down and cheeks pale, asleep against the mound of pillows.

Her maid glanced up from where she was sewing near the fire, but Mary smiled, shaking her head. It wouldn't do to wake the girl up from her nap, only to have her say her head hurt too much for reading.

Besides, Mary told herself as she crept back across the floor, *if Lady Anne wanted a novel, she could read the one Lord Sanders had bought her last year.*

She opened the door and stepped into the corridor, softly closing it behind her. Turning for the stairs, she collided with someone tall and firm, his arms going around her as they spun to the floor.

Wind knocked from her lungs, her cheek rested against the thundering heartbeat of...great. Lord Sanders, again. Squeezing her eyes closed against her embarrassment, Mary tried to ignore how warm he felt below her, how strong his arms had to be to help lift her while he lay on the floor. Disentangling herself from his hold, she righted herself and stepped back, pulling at her sleeves and straightening her skirts.

"Now this time I cannot take any of the blame," he said, a smile in his voice.

Mary couldn't help but chuckle, her cheeks flooding hot. "You could have avoided it by refraining from materializing out of nowhere."

"I was coming to check on my sister, and I needed to hurry. We are supposed to be meeting downstairs now."

She stepped toward the stairs, and he followed. "I just checked on Lady Anne, and she is sleeping."

"We mustn't bother her, then."

"My thoughts as well."

Mary tried to compose herself, but she could not deny what she had just felt in Lord Sanders's arms—the warmth which had flooded her body, the fluttering of her heart. She wanted to assume it was the natural response to being held by a man. She had felt similarly when they'd collided at the Frost Fair and when he'd caught her before she fell into the fire when they played the smiling game. But this was different. This time, Lord Sanders clutched her to his chest tightly and she *knew* he did not want to release her. His reluctance was startling, but she understood.

She'd felt the same hesitation to stand, to pull herself away from him.

Swallowing her inappropriate thoughts, Mary made it to the entryway.

"Have you seen Andrew?" Lady Caroline asked as she stood near the front door, pulling on her gloves, Miss Bolton waiting calmly behind her.

Mary glanced over her shoulder to find the earl coming down the stairs at a much slower pace, his gaze darting everywhere but her face. She put her back to him, training a bright smile on Lady Caroline and the girl's governess.

She would do what she needed to get over the earl, and she would be quick about it. If he chose to pretend nothing happened, that a current of longing did not run between them, then she would do the same.

Besides, what choice did she have?

CHAPTER 18

$\mathcal{H}$atchard's was the haven Andrew needed, with its shelves upon shelves of books spreading over multiple floors. The roaring fire in the fireplace surrounded by dark wood-paneled walls gave the shop a comforting, homey feel. The only difference between his library at home and Hatchard's Bookshop was that this building housed many books he had never before read. Anticipation burst within him; he could hardly wait to get his hands on a new, unread story.

But where to begin?

Caroline and Mary admired the books set in the window display before asking the shop worker to show them toward the novels they might enjoy. He led them away with a smile, Caroline's governess meandering behind them. Andrew could hear them discussing books and options with the clerk as he perused the shelves. He had been in this shop just a fortnight before and had purchased enough books to last him through the new year and past January. If only Anne enjoyed reading as he did, then he would have someone in the house to talk with about literature after Mary left them.

He paused near the base of the curved staircase, listening as Caroline and Mary spoke quietly together above him. He could not understand what they were saying, but he enjoyed hearing them, nonetheless.

Mary's voice reminded him of the hot chocolate they'd enjoyed at Gunter's earlier in the week—had that really been nearly a week ago? —warm, smooth, and delightful. Her attention, soft and encouraging, was exactly what a girl of twelve needed. Caroline spoke freely with Mary, unafraid of censure or reproach. Many adults were kind to younger people, and Andrew knew that, but Mary appeared more than just kind to Caroline. She appeared interested, as if she was perfectly content to spend the day speaking to a young, impressionable girl and share in the conversation.

Andrew left them to their perusal, slowly walking the various rooms of the bookshop as the women chatted upstairs. When they finally made their appearance, he helped them to the clerk's desk. Caroline laid her book on the counter, and Andrew waited for Mary to do the same. He could not give her much—nay, he did not have it in his power to shower her with praise and gifts as he would like to do— but he could do this one small thing for her. He could purchase her book.

"I believe I will spend the rest of the day reading," Caroline said, shooting a look at her governess, who stood demurely behind Mary. Miss Bolton gave the girl a reassuring nod, and Caroline beamed. "The family is shipwrecked in this book, Andrew. Can you imagine such a fate?"

The clerk cleared his throat behind the desk and Andrew glanced to Mary's hands, surprised to find them empty. "You did not find anything interesting, Miss Hatcher?"

"Oh," she said, startled. Her cheeks bloomed with color, making her otherwise pale complexion rosy. "I just—no, I did not. Not today."

She was embarrassed, and she was lying. Andrew debated pressing the matter, but the way Mary dropped her lashes and stepped away gave him pause.

"Not true," Caroline said. "You told me you would love to read *Evelina*."

Mary's blush deepened, and Andrew longed to brush his fingers over her warm cheeks and soothe away her embarrassment. She toyed with the reticule on her wrist, and it occurred to him that perhaps she might not have the funds to buy a book. They were expensive, and she had confessed her father's ruin to him only days ago.

"Perhaps later. Why should I buy any today when your brother has a library full of books I've not yet read? I can purchase *Evelina* next time."

"Or you may purchase it today to take home with you. It could help pass the time in the carriage when we travel home next week."

Next week? Shock coursed through Andrew's limbs, freezing him in place. Surely the women would not return home so soon.

Mary retreated further, her steps backing her away from Caroline as she softly shook her head. "Not today, Lady Caroline. But I thank you for your sweetness. I am eager to learn what you make of your new story, however."

Caroline's face brightened. But then her eyebrows drew together. "But surely—"

"Caroline," Andrew said, hoping he balanced authority in his tone with kind rebuke. She must learn when a subject was meant to be pressed, and when it ought to be dropped.

She seemed to take his meaning, however, for she said no more as the clerk accepted the money from Andrew and wrapped their package in brown paper and twine. Their party moved toward the door, bracing themselves for the cold, and Andrew held it open for the women to precede him outside. Mary paused on the walkway before the shop, Caroline nearly running into her, and elicited a small gasp.

"Mr. Lockhart!"

Andrew's body clenched, and he dropped the door, letting it swing closed after he and Miss Bolton had passed through it. The cold rushed up, assaulting his exposed skin, and prickling his nostrils.

Mr. Lockhart paused on the walkway ahead of them and glanced over his shoulder, a woman on his arm. His eyes lit on Mary, and he seemed to freeze as if the snow falling lazily around him had molded him in place. But as quickly as he froze, he thawed. He said something to the woman on his arm, and they turned together.

Andrew stepped forward, coming to a halt directly behind Mary.

"Miss Hatcher, what a fortuitous circumstance." Mr. Lockhart's eyes were unblinking, set on Mary. "What are you doing out in this wretched weather?"

"We have just been browsing books in Hatchard's, and I believe now we will return home to thaw."

"Of course, of course," Mr. Lockhart said. He cleared his throat, his gaze darting to Andrew and then back to Mary. "Please, allow me to introduce Mrs. Dobson, the widow of a friend of mine from Portsmouth." He turned to her. "And this is Lord Sanders, the Earl of Sanders, Lady Caroline, his sister, and Miss Hatcher, my betrothed."

The woman's dark eyes glanced to each of them in turn, and she dropped into a curtsy. Her thick, violet cloak and matching bonnet covered what appeared to be rich, auburn hair, and her cheeks, dusted with freckles, were red from the cold.

"We've only just come from Floris around the corner," Mrs. Dobson said. "I had a need for new perfume, and Mr. Lockhart was kind enough to escort me."

"How generous of you," Mary said, earning a smile from Mr. Lockhart, though her voice was stiff.

"I intended to call on you this afternoon and inquire after Lady Anne. Is she much improved?"

Mary nodded. "Yes, and the doctor believes she shall be fit for dancing by Twelfth Night."

"How relieved she must be," Mr. Lockhart said. "I hope to claim one of those dances myself."

As the young lady in question was not there to accept the request, no more was said on the matter of dancing. But Andrew couldn't help but think of the vase of expensive hothouse roses Mr. Lockhart had sent to Anne, and how she had refused to allow them into her room. When he'd questioned her on the matter she had refused to provide a reason, merely stating that she didn't want the flowers or their strong scent to heighten her headache.

He'd believed her, but now he wondered what she would say about dancing with the gentleman. If he just came from the perfume shop, would he carry a strong scent likely to heighten her headache as well?

"We must be off," Lord Sanders said, hoping he did not appear rude. "I must get these women out of the cold."

Mr. Lockhart nodded in agreement. The streets were still somewhat empty, the usually bustling roads only carrying a small fraction of the people it was used to. It was much too cold to stand around in this way for much longer.

"We hope to see you soon, Mr. Lockhart," Mary said, to her credit. "And I hope you stay warm," she added, looking to Mrs. Dobson.

"I shall, I thank you." Mrs. Dobson glanced at Mr. Lockhart, turning with him after he'd raised his hat to them, and they walked away.

Silence reigned over their party as they climbed into the waiting carriage and traveled home. Caroline unwrapped her book and examined the binding, the title page, the embossed title. She was silent, likely entranced with the prospect of a new story—something Andrew understood quite well.

But while his heart warmed over their shared interest in reading, his gaze could not help but stray toward Mary, her furrowed brow creasing worry lines on her forehead as she watched out the foggy, snow-covered window. He knew she must be lost in thought, for the window was impossible to see through. He desperately wanted to ask her what troubled her, but not in front of Caroline or Miss Bolton.

When they arrived home, Andrew waited in the entryway for Caroline and Miss Bolton to begin moving upstairs, his young sister's nose already glued to the book in her hands, and then he put a staying hand on Mary's shoulder. Water droplets clung to the material, wetting his gloves, and he pulled at the fingers to remove them.

"Are you quite all right, Miss Hatcher? You've become very quiet."

Her eyes rounded. "Yes, of course."

It was not *of course* to him, or he wouldn't have asked. "You are certain?" he pressed. "I am quite adept at keeping secrets."

Her smile was warm, though her nose and cheeks still looked red from the cold. "I know."

Andrew dropped his head to the side, running his gloves through his bare hand. "How?"

"You've never told anyone of your father's special deliveries, have you?" Her grin widened, growing sincere. "Well, until you told me."

"Ah, yes. I suppose you can trust me for a total of fifteen years, and then I just may forget and dump your secrets on unsuspecting strangers."

"I am a stranger?"

"Of course not."

She lifted an eyebrow, and he wanted to divulge just how familiar she had become to him, how he recognized the smell of the perfume she used, or how he was captivated by the familiar gleam in her eyes, how she was quick to smile and prompt to listen. "I only meant that I shared my father's secret, and you are a stranger to him."

"It is funny because I understand that I've never met him, but I feel as if I know him well from yours and your sisters' stories." Her face lit up, mouth opening in a small gasp. "I have just the thing! What if we were to continue your father's tradition, but bring your sisters into the scheme? We have a few days left before we leave Town. Surely that is enough time."

He enjoyed watching her expression shift as she thought through the concept. He nodded. "Yes, I am certain there is enough time."

A delighted smile played on her lips. "We can do something for the family Dr. Kent spoke of with the sick father."

"They are not poor," Andrew said.

"The rich do not struggle or find themselves in need of friendship and support, too?"

"No, of course they do, I only meant that my father's scheme was designed to help those in need."

She smiled at Andrew, resting her hand on his forearm. "I believe this family is in need, and a small package left on their doorstep will likely feed their emotional needs right now more than their physical ones. Sometimes it is just enough to know that someone is thinking of us."

"That is true, isn't it?"

"And perhaps we can assemble some baskets to deliver to an orphanage, or another family you may know in the area with more pressing physical needs."

"We can bring Anne and Caroline into this decision, but I do like the idea of the orphanage."

Mary released his arm, much to his disappointment, and turned for the stairs. "I will check on Anne after I put away my bonnet and things. If she is awake, shall we begin planning?"

Andrew nodded. His throat wasn't working properly, and he was afraid his voice would sound awkward and raspy if he spoke, but Mary didn't seem to notice as she shot him a smile and began ascending the stairs.

Andrew's legs wouldn't move as he stood in the entryway, light streaming from the windows behind him and casting his shadow on the floor ahead of him. Mary's kind thoughtfulness reached a peak, rivaling her beauty as the most striking of her features. She was intelligent, she was selfless, and Andrew was in a spot of trouble. Because despite her utter perfection, she was unavailable.

And he was in love with her.

CHAPTER 19

$\mathcal{M}$ary sat in a tufted chair pulled close to Lady Anne's bedside, a small writing desk to her left. Dipping the quill, she paused, looking over the note she had penned wishing the Bartlett family a Happy Christmas. "What shall I sign the note?"

Lady Anne's nose crinkled. "Perhaps we ought to leave it blank."

"Or we could sign it, 'Affectionately, your friends?'"

"But *are* we their friends? I've never heard of this family before now, despite Mrs. Bartlett being a cousin to Lady Rutledge."

"No, but we could be." Had it only been yesterday that they'd gone to the bookstore and decided to take a box to this family? Mary had never met the Bartletts before, but she was concerned about their wellbeing. "And we care for their plight, so I do not find it dishonest to sign the note from their friends."

Lady Anne nodded. She sat up in her bed, pushing another pillow behind her. "I am ready to leave this room. When are we delivering the box?"

"Your brother would like to go this evening if you are feeling up for it. Or tomorrow, if you'd prefer to wait another day."

"No, let us go this evening. Now that my blasted headache has eased, I feel fit enough for an outing."

Mary raised her eyebrows, but Lady Anne didn't seem to notice anything amiss. Her language could not have come from her mother or her governess, so Mary assumed it had to be blamed on the girl's brother.

A knock at the door preceded Lord Sanders, and he stepped into the room, coming to pause at the foot of Anne's bed. "The boxes are prepared."

"And the note is nearly finished," Mary said, focusing on the letters as she penned them. She set down her pen and turned in her seat to face the earl. "And Caroline?"

"She is still up in her room reading her new book. She requested that we send for her when it is time to leave. We could probably wait until tomorrow night and Caroline would not notice."

Lady Anne scoffed. "You think she could read clear until tomorrow night and not realize a day had passed?"

Lord Sanders looked to Mary, a smile quirking his lips. "Yes, I do."

Lady Anne sunk against her pillows. "I will never understand that."

Her brother chuckled. "Perhaps if you opened a book, Anne, you would understand. Just ask Mary. She read the book I got you last year, and vastly enjoyed it."

"It is true," Mary said gravely, eliciting a laugh from Lady Anne. "Are we planning to go out following dinner?"

"That was my thought." The earl folded his arms over his chest.

"What do we tell the mothers?"

"I assumed we'd tell them the truth," Lord Sanders said. "I can take care of it before dinner."

"Should we invite them along?" Mary asked.

Lord Sanders gave her a smile. "I have a feeling they will prefer to remain home, but I will be sure to extend the invitation." He turned to leave but paused at the door. "I will see you both at dinner."

His heavy footsteps could be heard as he retreated down the corridor then closed a door behind himself.

"I never did ask what you purchased at the book store," Lady Anne said. "But in my defense, I have not quite been myself these last few days. I don't believe I've ever slept so much in my life."

"There is nothing wrong with that. I heard the doctor recommend sleep as an aide in battling your headache."

"Then you forgive me? Now do tell me what you chose. I'm sure I've never heard of it, but one never knows."

Mary chuckled, slipping her fingers down the silky feather at the end of her pen. "I did not purchase a book."

Lady Anne's face contorted. "But you love to read just as much as my brother does."

"And I have plenty of books. Now, will you explain why I found that lovely bouquet of roses out in the corridor? Have you taken a dislike to flowers since you hit your head?"

She stilled, her face going pale, and her expression caused a thread of alarm to bind Mary's chest. "What is it?" Mary asked.

Lady Anne dropped her gaze, her fingers playing with the edge of her blanket. "Nothing, exactly. I only thought I saw something the other night, but it was late and those lamps on the street really do not cast a decent light, do they?"

"What was it?" Mary pressed. She had thought it silly when she found those roses in the corridor, but now she was concerned.

"I saw Mr. Lockhart—or, well, I *thought* I saw Mr. Lockhart outside the hotel when we arrived, and he was with a woman."

"A woman?" Mary's heart beat a hasty pattern. She told herself it was nothing, but her body refused to listen.

"Yes. They were walking together. She wore a violet cloak that was very fine, and Mr. Lockhart—"

"A violet cloak? Well, surely that was Mrs. Dobson. We met her yesterday at the bookstore."

Lady Anne looked confused. "With Mr. Lockhart?"

"Yes, they had gone to Floris together to purchase perfume. She is the widow of a dear friend of Mr. Lockhart's from Portsmouth."

"Oh, I am so unbelievably relieved!" Anne said, dropping her head back and sighing. She glanced up, wide-eyed. "I was so worried, and I hadn't the faintest notion of how to tell you what I saw."

"He was merely being a gentleman, but I am grateful for your friendship and concern. Now, I better go and change for dinner. I will see you downstairs tonight, yes?"

"Yes, I will be there."

Mary stood to go, maintaining her composure as she left the room. But Lady Anne's words stayed with her as she climbed the stairs to the next floor and went into her own chamber, closing the door softly behind her and sitting on the edge of the bed. She did not have cause for concern, not when all Lady Anne had seen was Mr. Lockhart and Mrs. Dobson walking alone together. Mary had seen that very same thing yesterday, and it had appeared completely innocent.

Yet there was this niggling at the back of her mind, tugging at her and warning her. The expression Mr. Lockhart had worn when his gaze had fallen on her was so quick, such a flash of panic, that she wondered if she had seen it in reality or merely imagined it.

His expression flashed in her mind again, and it was unmistakable. Dread pooled around her, closing in and squeezing her chest, making it difficult to draw a breath. There was something between Mr. Lockhart and the widow, something that he did not want her to see. But if he was hiding a woman from Mary, what could that mean?

He had not given any indication of harboring a wish to break their engagement, and Mary was in no position to do so. What would her father do to repay the debts? Mr. Lockhart had made it perfectly clear: if the marriage did not occur between them, or if Mary did not maintain her end of the bargain and find her betrothed an entry into the *ton*, then he would call in Father's debts and send him to prison. There was no other recourse for her, and there was nothing she could do.

Reality slammed on Mary, and she shut her eyes, pressing her fingers to her temples. Drawing in a deep breath, she let it out slowly, counting as she did so to calm her racing heart. She would marry Mr. Lockhart, she would obtain the invitation from the Brights to their summer house party, and then she would retire to Berkshire and live out the rest of her days in solitude, hopefully finding some companionship in her new mother-in-law.

Opening her eyes again, she sat up straight, determined. She could do all of these things, of course, but she deserved not to be blindsided by whatever it was that Mr. Lockhart was hoping to keep from her. She had only a handful of days left in London before they returned to Berkshire, and she would use that time to discover what she could.

CHAPTER 20

*a*ndrew's mother believed their plan to deliver a box of Cook's fresh gingerbread with a kind note and oranges to the Bartlett family was splendid, but she in no way wished to partake in the outing, and Mrs. Hatcher soundly agreed. They had a surprise for the children that they were planning to present to them the following day, but they needed to add the finishing touches.

Whatever that could possibly mean.

Andrew met Caroline, Anne, and Mary in the library after dinner, their winter cloaks, gloves, and muffs prepared and ready for their departure.

"This is exciting!" Anne said, a brilliant smile on her face. The last three days of rest had done wonders for her, and she did not appear any worse for having taken the fall outside of the Clarendon Hotel. "Am I supposed to feel such anticipation?"

"I would think so," Caroline said. "Though I've never done anything so clandestine before."

"It is the thrill of doing our utmost not to get caught," Andrew explained, coming to stop before the sofa of excited women. "Shall we deliver the orphanage boxes first? Or the Bartletts'?"

"I would like to do the orphanage one first. I do hope the children are awake."

"It won't matter," Anne argued. "It is not as if we'll be able to witness their reaction."

Caroline seemed to consider this, tiny lines forming between her eyebrows. "That hadn't occurred to me."

Mary rose, taking a step back to avoid colliding with Andrew. "Shall we?"

"Yes, let's be off."

They filed downstairs and out into the cold, dark night. The servants had loaded one end of a bench in the carriage with the boxes and the interior of the vehicle smelled of warm gingerbread, despite the chilly evening. Mary sat between the sisters, Andrew opposite them, and he could not help but feel as if something was off.

Mary had not been rude, but she seemed distant. It was strange behavior, and nothing like he was used to seeing from her in the short few weeks he'd known her. They rode along the bumpy London streets until they rolled to a stop, and Andrew looked at each of the women.

"Who shall deliver the first box?"

"Not Anne," Caroline said. "We don't want to risk her falling again."

Anne scowled at her sister, but Andrew noticed that she did not disagree with this. "Caroline, would you like to go first? I can come along if you wish."

She smiled, and he could see her teeth gleaming, the faint light from the building casting a glow on them through their window.

Caroline and Andrew climbed out of the carriage and up the steps toward the orphanage. She set the box at the base of the door and looked up at him. "And now what do we do?"

"We knock," he whispered. "Would you like to?"

She shook her head. "I am afraid of falling."

He chuckled but waited until she made it down the slick stairs before knocking on the door and hurrying to his carriage. Light spilled onto the steps as the front door opened, but Andrew's coachman had taken off the moment he closed his door, and they would probably not be recognized in the dark.

"That was immensely satisfying!" Caroline said, and Mary smiled. "Can we do it again?"

"Yes. We have two more orphanages to stop at."

The warmth within the carriage grew and expounded as the small party continued on their way, leaving boxes of gingerbread and oranges at the next two orphanages. The coachman drove them to the Bartletts' house, and they found themselves stopped in front of a white stone townhouse, the streets well lit—when compared to those belonging to the orphanages—and the area clean.

The carriage continued around the corner of the building as Andrew had instructed, so they might sneak away if the servants were close enough to open the door quickly.

"Would you like to take this box?" Andrew asked, looking at Mary. She had remained within the carriage during the previous three drop-offs with Anne, but this particular house had been her idea.

"I certainly can," she said, reaching for the box in his hands.

He held it strong. "I can come with you. Caroline?"

She shook her head. "I will watch this one."

Andrew stepped out first, then took Mary's hand, helping her onto the frozen ground. They walked in silence up the walkway and around the corner, their footprints following them in the snow until they reached the correct townhouse and mounted the steep stone steps to the front door. Andrew placed the box on the ground before the door. "Would you like to knock, or shall I?"

She gazed up at him, her eyes latching onto his with a fierceness he had not expected. Shaking her head slowly, she sighed, and her breath clouded between them. He was grateful for the cover of dark-ness, that he had the ability to stare at her unhindered, to watch her large, round eyes look at him as though she was looking into his soul.

Her voice, soft and stripped of any effect, went straight to his heart. "Do you see now what an incredible man you are?"

Andrew stood still, stunned, as Mary knocked on the door and turned, fleeing down the steps. His brain caught up a moment later, and he raced after her, leaping around the corner as the door opened, flooding orange light onto the steps where they had been just a moment ago.

Ducking behind a shrubbery at the corner, he took Mary's arm and pulled her down beside him. In the shadows away from the street lamps and the lights from the houses, they disappeared, their dark coats blending into the shrubs.

He held her flush against his side, doing his best to steady her as they both peered over the top of the bush and watched a woman in a plain serving gown bend down and retrieve the box in the snow. She glanced up, her gaze sweeping the street, and they ducked lower, hiding.

"What does delivering boxes have to do with the type of man I am?" he whispered, his mouth so close to Mary that he could almost feel her ear against his lips. She shuddered in his arms, and he hoped it was from him and not the cold.

"You are not unintelligent, Andrew," she whispered back. "I mean, my lord...you know exactly what I meant. You are continuing your father's tradition, bringing Caroline and Anne into something they never got to experience."

He smiled. "Anne did do this with my father, but she never told me, and I never told her."

Mary turned to look in his face, and he froze. She was so close now he could lean forward, and his lips would touch hers. "Because you both kept your father's secret."

"Exactly."

"Then I amend my comment. You are bringing Caroline into something she never before got to experience. And with the way she has utterly latched on to you the last few days, I am certain you would agree that she has vastly enjoyed your company."

"I am not sure this is an argument you will win, Mary, but if you would like to continue talking about it, I am willing."

"My toes are frozen."

"I have a remedy for that as well."

She lifted her eyebrows, and Andrew glanced at the Bartletts' house. The front steps were dark again, the danger of being caught well past, and he rose, pulling Mary to her feet beside him. The cold rushed in on him with greater force, and he took her hand, pulling her toward the carriage. She did not resist him. Instead, her fingers tightened over his, and it sent a shock straight up his arm.

He led her to the carriage and helped her inside but felt as though Mary was avoiding his gaze.

"That took quite a long time," Anne said.

"We were nearly caught." Andrew settled onto the bench beside Mary, across from his sisters. There was adequate room now that the boxes had been removed.

"What an adventure. Do you think they saw you?"

"No," Mary said. "But we ducked behind the hedgerow just in time or they might have. Not that they would have had any idea who I was, but I am certain your brother is easily recognizable."

"Perhaps," Andrew conceded. He'd been living in London for the better part of the last five years. And most of that he'd been alone. It struck him as odd that the idea of living in Sanders House once his mother and sisters returned to Brightly Court in Cheshire, he might find himself lonely in London by himself. He hadn't felt that way before though, so it was likely an odd notion that would certainly pass.

The quiet would be welcome. He would have the luxury of reading far more often, at least.

"That was exhilarating," Caroline said, her voice betraying her enthusiasm. "I do hope we will do that again next year."

"I don't see any reason why we couldn't," Andrew said. The carriage jostled them to the side, and Mary nearly fell into him. He put his arm up for her to hold, and she grasped his elbow, using it to steady herself.

"Well, if we do not return to London for Christmas, then that might pose a problem." Caroline's voice brightened again. "But perhaps we could do it during the summer when you come to Brightly for the house party!"

Andrew's guilt deepened the more Caroline innocently tried to create plans. Her life had been a pattern of only seeing Andrew during the summer house party, and occasionally on Christmas, so why should he expect her to think differently? He hardly saw her otherwise, unless his mother chose to come to London for the Season, but that had been sporadic.

Anne yawned. "What do you think our mothers are doing up in that parlor? They have been so secretive."

Mary chuckled. "I think we will soon find out."

"We must," Anne said. "We leave in three days."

Three? "So soon?"

"Mother wants to return to Brightly, and the Hatchers need to return home. Mary's wedding is only a fortnight away."

Mary's fingers tightened on his sleeve, and then she released him as if realizing what her hands were doing. Anne continued talking about all they needed to do to prepare to travel back to the countryside, but Andrew wasn't paying her any mind. His thoughts were wrapped around an image of Mary standing at the front of a church beside Mr. Lockhart. His body revolted.

He could not allow her to think she must marry that man in order to save her father. Not if her heart was not engaged. Andrew had enough money to pay the man back his debts. As Mary's Godmother, Andrew's mother had some stake in her wellbeing. Certainly it would be acceptable to come to an agreement that would satisfy all parties.

She had said herself she was not in love with Mr. Lockhart.

"It is too bad we did not know you better years ago, Mary," Anne said wistfully as the carriage arrived back at Sanders House. "I would have loved to spend Christmas with you every year."

"Indeed," Andrew agreed. "I can think of more than one reason I would have liked to have known you better years ago."

Namely, that he might have offered for her first.

Mary looked at him sharply and he held her gaze in the dark, only light from the lamps shining on her eyes. The door swung open and Andrew stepped out of the carriage, turning to help the women down. Anne looked tired, her face paler than normal, and he allowed her to lean on his arm as Caroline and Mary walked ahead of them.

"I am only tired," Anne explained, leaning heavily as they took the stairs up to each new floor. They were nearly there now, and the other women had gone on ahead and disappeared.

"You suffered a blow, Anne. It is perfectly reasonable to take more time to heal. Think nothing of it."

She turned anxious eyes on him. "But the ball. It is only two days away, and I am exhausted after sitting in the carriage for an evening and watching the three of you have all the excitement. How am I supposed to dance all night?"

"I have complete faith in you. You will dance, and you will rest when you need it." He squeezed her shoulders. "And you will enjoy the ball."

A smile lit up her face and she crushed into Andrew, her slender arms wrapping him in an embrace. "You always know just the thing to say to calm my nerves. I do not know how I was so blessed to have you for a brother."

Shock rippled through his limbs, and he returned her hug, pulling her close. "I love you, Anne."

She stepped back, smiling at him. "I love you too, Andrew."

Anne went into her room. He stood outside her door for a few minutes considering her words. Perhaps he was not—nor ever would be—the perfect brother. But his sisters seemed receptive to what little he could do.

Taking the stairs down toward the library, he was stopped in the hallway by Finch.

"You've got visitors."

"This late?"

"They only just arrived. Mr. Pinnegar and Mr. Jacobs, my lord. I've placed them in the library."

Ah, of course. Last he'd heard from either of them was a week ago, at least, and he'd sent Harold away in order to spend time with his sisters and Mary. He was sorely tempted to do the same thing again, but that wouldn't be kind.

No, he could manage a short visit with his friends. But then he would set his mind to the dilemma with Mary and her father's debts, her marriage contract with Mr. Lockhart, and what Andrew might do to fix it all to his liking.

He made his way downstairs, certain they were only here to do their best to convince him to come out with them for a night of Faro or to drink at one of their clubs. He could easily put them off.

But when he stepped into the library Andrew had not expected to find Mary amongst them.

CHAPTER 21

$\mathcal{L}$ord Sanders's friends were curious men with playful dispositions. Mary was able to surmise that from the short few minutes she'd spent in their company. That she heartily wished to be *removed* from said company mattered little, for she did not know how to extricate herself without being rude. If only the earl would arrive soon, then she could leave him to his friends and slip quietly from the room.

"You are a friend of the family's?" the blonde one asked, his smile wide, like a cat preparing to pounce.

"Indeed," Lord Sanders's deep voice said from the doorway. He surveyed the scene, settling his gaze momentarily on Mary before looking to his friends. "And while I'm sure you were waiting for me to introduce you, I am not certain an introduction should take place. I owe this woman my utmost discretion when introducing her to wretched men."

"Doing it too brown, I say." The red-haired man's smile betrayed his amusement. "We are perfectly appropriate acquaintances for any young woman to have."

Lord Sanders lifted an eyebrow, standing at the edge of the sofa where his friends were both seated, Mary standing behind the wing-back chair opposite them, her hands folded over the top of the chair.

"I'm not sure about that, but since Miss Hatcher is a woman who knows her own mind and possesses the intelligence to sniff out rats"—he pierced his friends with a glare—" then I am going to trust you not to say anything you might later regret."

They both nodded.

The earl cleared his throat. "Miss Hatcher, allow me to present friends of mine, Mr. Harold Pinnegar and Mr. Francis Jacobs."

She dipped into a curtsy, and the men both rose, bowing. "Pleased. But I don't wish to impose. If you will only allow me a moment to select a book, I will shortly be out of your hair."

"Please, take all the time you need," Lord Sanders said with a generous smile. He waited until she stepped away from the group to take his seat on a wingback chair, and she moved to the bookcase behind him where they had previously found *Pride & Prejudice*.

Scanning the titles on the case, she tuned out the low conversation being held near the fire. She only had two full days left at Sanders House and then they planned to travel home. The weather was not ideal, but it had mellowed enough to make the trip possible. Each of the women in the house was ready to return to the country, and Mary told herself she should feel the same.

It was not as though she did not love her home in Berkshire. But the last few weeks in London had been some of the happiest of her life, and she was loath to see them come to an end.

Particularly when it occurred to her that they could never repeat these happy days again, for, in just a little longer than a fortnight, she would become Mrs. Lockhart.

A shudder wracked her shoulders, and she returned her focus to the books. When her eyes fell on a collection of Shakespeare plays, she pulled the large, heavy tome from the shelf. If she only had a few days, she could lose herself in a familiar story, one that she might finish when she returned home using her own copy.

But only in the daytime, of course. The lamps and candles she'd used here to read late into the night were an expense she was not fortunate enough to indulge in at home. At least, not until her marriage finalized.

Pausing at the edge of the rug, she wrapped her arms around the book and smiled at the men. They each stood upon her approach. "Forgive my intrusion, my lord, Mr. Pinnegar, Mr. Jacobs."

"You are forgiven, Miss Hatcher," Mr. Pinnegar said. "I am only sorry we did not have the opportunity for a deeper acquaintanceship."

She held his gaze a moment before she nodded and turned to leave.

Footsteps followed her from the room, and she paused just outside the door, glancing back to find Lord Sanders just behind her.

"Did you wish to read in here?" His voice was low, meant for her ears alone, and despite the bland topic, it gave her a thrill. "I can take them to the drawing room."

"No," she said, a smile coming unbidden to her lips. He was the most thoughtful man. "I am happy to return upstairs. I hadn't expected anyone to be in the library or I wouldn't have bothered your guests."

He leaned in a little, his eyebrows raising a fraction. "I believe *you* are the guest who was bothered today."

"Not in the slightest. They only wished for an introduction before you arrived, and I refused to perform it myself. I do not blame their curiosity at finding an unknown woman in their friend's home. Did you not tell them your mother had guests?"

"I did tell them, but I refrained from expounding on how lovely those guests were. You've successfully piqued their interest."

She drew in a quick breath. Had the earl realized what he'd said? She imagined so, given the intense look in his blue eyes, and her heart refused to slow. "My mother would be gratified by your praise."

He shot her a wry smile. "What book did you choose?"

She lifted it, moving her arms away from the title.

"Ah," he said. "A classic. Which one will you read?"

"I was thinking *Twelfth Night*, actually. It seems fitting."

His smile was as soft as his voice. "I do hope you enjoy it. Good-night, Miss Hatcher."

She dipped her head and turned to go up the stairs. Lord Sanders had upended her equilibrium though, and her head spun. What had caused this change in behavior? He'd been so politely distant for the duration of their visit, never putting her in a position to feel uncomfortable. Every stray thought she'd had or attraction she'd felt over the last fortnight was entirely her own fault, her own feelings.

But tonight? Something had shifted between them. He had praised her, followed her into the corridor heedless of what his friends might think or say. He was emboldened, and she wanted to know why.

Because despite her understanding that there could never be something between the earl and herself, her dreams hoped otherwise.

Francis leaned back in his seat, crossing his ankle over the opposite knee, his head gesturing toward the door. "You've been keeping *that* secret well-hidden."

Andrew ignored his friend, settling back in his chair.

Harold put a staying hand on Francis's shoulder. "Don't press him, man. He will explain when he's ready."

"There's nothing to explain." Andrew hoped his voice sounded even, that he was not betraying his lie.

"Is that what you've been doing the last few weeks? And here I thought your mother wanted your companionship."

"She requested I make myself present for my sisters. Her guests have had nothing to do with it."

"Why does her name sound familiar?" Francis asked, screwing up his mouth in thought. "I know I've heard it recently, and it wasn't in this house."

Lord Sanders frowned. "She's from Berkshire and doesn't come out in Society here. Perhaps you heard of different Hatchers."

Harold snapped his fingers. "I know it. We heard it from the steps of Boodles the other night. A gentleman was trying to obtain entry, and they blocked him at the door."

Francis sat up. "The dandy? I remember this. He lacked an introduction and made a fuss. No one knew his name, so of course they were not going to let him in."

"Yes. But do you recall his argument with the doorman? He said he was engaged to Miss Mary Hatcher as if that would hold any weight." Harold guffawed, showing his teeth. "No one in the vicinity had even heard her name before."

"Until now," Francis added, grinning. "My, she *is* lovely. You think the dandy from Boodles is marrying her with a false idea of her rank? He did call her a *miss*, so he cannot be wholly fooled into believing she holds a title."

"Her mother's grandfather was an earl," Andrew explained. "She does have entry into the *ton* should she wish it, but I believe her family has largely kept to themselves. My mother is her godmother, you know, and our families' connection runs clear back to our mothers' childhoods. Their own parents were dear friends."

Harold sat up. "You are awfully defensive of Miss Hatcher's claim to a respectable connection, Sanders."

He shrugged. "I don't wish for her name to be dragged through the mud when she has done nothing to earn it. I've met with Mr. Lockhart and Miss Hatcher together on numerous occasions, and she has done nothing to indicate that she is misleading him in any capacity."

Indeed, the very thought of Lockhart shouting her name for all to hear at Boodles, subjecting her to conversations such as this across London's drawing rooms, made him ill.

Francis lifted his hands in defense. "Your issue is with this Lockhart fellow, Sanders. We are merely the messengers."

"Perhaps you ought to let your Miss Hatcher know what is being said," Harold added. "She seems a nice enough woman. She might appreciate being warned about her husband's actions. He created quite a scene."

"He is not her husband," Andrew said, his tone steel.

"*Yet*," Harold said. They watched one another, the silence stretching, Harold seemingly trying to push Andrew into a confession with his eyes alone.

But he was going to be disappointed. Andrew might care about

Mary, but he was not about to tell his friends as much. It would be spread about London by morning if he did.

"Was that all?" Andrew asked.

Francis scoffed. "That's not even why we came."

"Another wager, then? Who bet this time that they could get me to leave my house?"

"No one," Harold said. "We just wanted to make sure you were still alive. That no one was forcing you to remain here against your will." He stood, sending his friend a victorious smile. "I believe we have confirmed that you are remaining here under your own free will and can therefore leave you in peace."

"How good of you," Andrew said drily. He stood, following his friends to the door. They bid him goodbye and slipped out into the cold, frozen night, but their words and warnings remained behind, crushing him.

He needed advice. Particularly that of a trusted friend...but his closest friend was all the way across the country. He sighed, pinching the bridge of his nose.

It was moments like these when Andrew wished most that his father was still around.

CHAPTER 22

$\mathcal{M}$ama and Lady Sanders sat through breakfast like a couple of schoolgirls, grinning and whispering to one another as their gazes darted between their children. Mary took the roll from her plate and sliced it open with her knife, spreading butter over the inside. It melted over the steaming bread and the yeasty smell was enough to tempt her to shove the entirety of the roll into her mouth. Instead, she broke off a small bite and put it in her mouth, doing her best to ignore the earl sitting across from her at the table, cutting into his ham and watching her from the corner of his eye.

Lady Sanders rose from the table, dropping her napkin on her plate. "We would like to see all of you in the drawing room when you've finished your breakfast. Say, half-past nine?"

"Of course, Mother," Lord Sanders said, standing until both of the mothers had risen and left the room. Once they were gone, he reclaimed his seat and returned to cutting into his slices of cold ham. "I wonder what they have planned for us," he said, staring at his ham.

"I have no idea what it could possibly be. But it has taken them nearly the duration of our visit to prepare, so we must be suitably grateful."

"Shall we practice our pleased expressions now, do you think?"

Mary chewed another bite of her roll. "That would probably be wise. You may begin."

Clearing his throat, Lord Sanders said. "Will you say something to me, and then I can react?"

"Of course." She sat back in her seat, resting her hands in her lap. "Your beard is so long, I would like to braid it."

Lord Sanders reared back, his face contorting into one of surprise mixed with disgust. Then a wide smile crept over his lips, and he threw his head back, laughter spilling forth.

Mary couldn't help but mirror him, laughter bubbling up from her chest and filling the breakfast room.

"I failed that test, did I not?" he asked, his eyes gleaming with unshed tears.

"Perhaps it was too much."

"Perhaps I won't shave tomorrow, and we will see what you think then."

Mary laughed, unable to help herself, her gaze skipping along his angular, clean-shaven jaw. "You might grow a beard if you wish. I cannot promise it will make it any easier for you to catch a woman's heart, however."

"Are women so fickle-minded that something as minor as a long, braidable beard would interfere with their affections?"

She lifted an eyebrow, and it was Lord Sanders's turn to laugh.

"Oh, good. I am famished," Lady Anne said, sweeping into the room and taking the seat beside Mary. Lady Caroline followed shortly behind her, sitting beside her brother and pulling a roll onto her plate. She busied herself with slathering butter on her bread, and Lady Anne spoke of the ball the following evening hosted by the esteemed Lady Rutledge.

"My gown has two layers of flounces, and I have set my maid to embroidering the toes of my slippers with deep red roses, so they match the embroidery on my gown. It is quite lovely together, but I cannot show you until tomorrow night." She took a bite of her breakfast and then continued, "I wouldn't want to ruin the effect, you know."

"Of course not," Lord Sanders agreed. "The element of surprise will add to the reveal, I should think."

Mary smiled as Lady Anne nodded emphatically. She snuck a look at the earl, his eyes gleaming with mirth. He was teasing his sister, but not in a mean-spirited way.

She sighed. She was absolutely going to miss this family when she left. Rising, she placed her napkin on the table. "I shall see you all in the drawing room soon."

The Bright siblings returned their attention to their meal and Mary left them, picking up the compilation of Shakespeare stories from the table where she'd left it and carrying it with her to the drawing room. The mothers hadn't arrived yet, so she made herself comfortable and flipped the book open to the page where she had left off.

But she could not focus. Her mind was running over the events of the previous day and how she had felt being held in Lord Sanders's arms when they'd hid behind the bush at the Bartletts' house. The warm safety his arms provided had been soothing, as though she could have closed her eyes and remained there forever and been perfectly content.

Voices down the hall preceded the mothers, and moments later they were letting themselves into the drawing room, large boxes in each of their arms and delighted smiles on their faces. They greeted Mary and then moved to set the boxes down on the floor beside the chairs in the circle of furniture before the fireplace, leaving one box at Mary's feet.

"Now, don't open it yet, dear," Mama said, bustling over to the settee and taking a seat beside her friend. "We want to wait for the others."

"Of course." But the size of the box was alarming, and Mary's stomach clenched. It was enormous, large enough to rival the boxes of gowns they'd been sent from the modiste's shop. But mother had not approached her for funds, and she clearly had none of her own.

Oh, dear. Had she thrown them further into debt?

"I hear them coming," Lady Sanders said, reaching for Mama and gripping her hands. "Can you believe we've wasted all these years apart?"

Mary looked up, glancing between the women.

Mama sighed. "I know, but I cannot help it. I simply hate leaving my home. It is so very uncomfortable for me."

"I knew this, though. I should have come to you more often," Lady Sanders said. "I plan to in the future, you know."

Lady Anne, Lady Caroline, and Lord Sanders stepped into the room, and their mother directed them to the appropriate seats, each of them sitting with a box at their feet. Mary's heart constricted. If her mother hadn't been so opposed to traveling, would Mary have grown up knowing the Bright children intimately? Lord Sanders had mentioned wishing he'd known Mary longer, that they might have spent more Christmases together. If he had come into her life before Mr. Lockhart had, who would she be engaged to now?

She shook the thought away, clenching her hands together on her lap. It would not do to reimagine the past. It was over now, and nothing could be done to change it.

"Are you ready?" Lady Sanders's wide smile matched Mama's.

A chorus of assent met her question, and she clapped her hands together. "Now, you might not all remember this, but when you were very little, we spent Christmas together at the Hatchers' house, and we had the most beautiful matching dresses made for the two of you"—she indicated Mary and Lady Anne with her hands—"in crimson *crêpe de Chine*, and the most handsome little matching waistcoat for Andrew. Sadly, Caro, you were not born yet. We had discussed making it a tradition, but that was the last time we spent Christmas together."

"Now, open your boxes," Mama said.

Lady Anne and Lady Caroline both bent, lifting the lids from their boxes to reveal matching forest green gowns with a deeper green embroidery about the hem. They gasped, pulling their gowns out of the boxes, and Mary's stomach wound tighter.

She looked up to find Andrew regarding her closely as if wondering why she had not yet opened her box; she finally leaned forward to do just that. Lifting the lid of the box, she revealed exactly what she had been afraid of finding—a matching gown to rival the grandeur and the cost of Lady Anne's and Lady Caroline's.

She swallowed against a dry throat, looking up at her mother. She could say nothing about the expense now, not when Mama watched her with such a warm smile and a serene, pleased glimmer in her eye.

Had the woman even known she was digging them further into debt? Mary thought it likely not.

"Andrew, what are you waiting for?" Lady Sanders asked.

"I was watching their faces," he explained, before turning to his own smaller box and lifting the lid to reveal a matching waistcoat with the same dark green embroidery, red berries strewn throughout.

Lady Anne lifted her gown, holding it against her torso. "However did you have these made so quickly?"

"They were completed within a few days, actually. We returned to the shop that made Mary's gowns and asked that these be put on priority in order to give us time to add the embroidery."

Mary lifted the hem of her gown, admiring the holly leaves and red berries. Her mother had done that for her? Surely that must have lessened the expense.

"Shall we all wear them today?" Lady Caroline asked.

"We had intended for them to be used for the ball, darling," Lady Sanders said. "I was hoping we could spend dinner together tomorrow with Caroline, and then you could all match."

"But, Mama, I had the rose gown made for the ball especially. I've even had my maid embroidering my slippers to match."

"Oh, well, you may wear whatever you wish, I suppose," Lady Sanders said, flustered. "We hadn't meant to force any of you, of course. It was just a thought."

"A lovely thought," Mary said, though her voice sounded stilted. "I shall carry mine upstairs this moment and see to it that Price knows to prepare it for the ball tomorrow."

"Oh, lovely, dear," Lady Sanders said, beaming. "I am so eager to see you all dressed for the ball. I wish it was tonight."

Mary closed the box and lifted it, hoping she did not appear awkward in the way she carried it. Usually she asked a servant to assist her, but now she needed an excuse to leave the room and gather her wits about her again. She would find a quiet moment with her mother later and learn how they were meant to pay for this gown. Perhaps she would have time tomorrow morning to sell her pearls and her ruby earbobs—that ought to cover a portion of the expense.

She reached the base of the stairs when she realized how very difficult it was going to be to see her feet and carry the box simultaneously. She was bound to trip over her skirt.

"Allow me," Lord Sanders said, sweeping to her side and taking the box smoothly from her arms.

"You really don't need to."

"I couldn't allow you to carry it upstairs by yourself." He said this as though it was purely sensical, and she allowed him to help her. She preceded him upstairs, her mind running wild, the fear of not being able to pay for the gown and the embarrassment it would cause her mother nearly undoing her.

Of course, she could always ask Mr. Lockhart for a small loan, but the very image that conjured in her mind was revolting, twisting her stomach in knots.

"What is it that is bothering you?"

"What do you mean?" she asked, pausing on the stairs. He could not see her face. How did he know she was bothered?

"I can feel it, Miss Hatcher. I don't know how I've gained this skill in the last fortnight, but I find I can sense your emotion right now, that your light is dimmer. That being said, will you turn, please, and face me?"

CHAPTER 23

It had been a bold request to ask Mary to turn around on the stairs and face him, but he'd needed to see her expression, to gauge what it was that bothered her, that took her swiftly from playful at the breakfast table to utterly distressed in the drawing room. To his utter delight, she spun slowly on the step until her serious, round eyes were fixed on him, her mouth closed in a firm line.

"What is it?" he asked again, quietly.

She shook her head. "I will bring shame and embarrassment upon my family if I am to tell you. I cannot."

"You must know by now that nothing you could say would deplete your standing in my eyes."

"You told me once that you are a curious man. How do I know you are not merely feeding that curiosity right now?"

He swallowed a scoff. "I wish to know because I care for you, not simply to appease my interest."

Mary turned and continued up the stairs, the skirt of the same gown she'd worn almost every morning that he'd seen her swishing at her heels. He followed quietly behind her until they reached the floor with her bedchamber. She paused at her door and held her hands out for the box, but he set it on the floor and took her hands in his own, her skin warm and soft in his.

Her eyes widened at his touch, her expression wary.

"Please, lighten your burden. I only wish to help."

She stared at their hands clasped in between them, soft lines forming on her brow. "I believe I told you once that my mother has largely been kept in the dark regarding our financial burdens. She has a fragile disposition, you see, and we must take care of her. But what I fear is that she has overextended our purse in the purchasing of this gown, and I haven't the slightest notion how I am to make up the difference." She looked up into his eyes, concern lining the depths of hers, pools of emerald he very well could get lost in. "I don't wish to embarrass her, but I don't see how I can wear that gown until I have resolved this."

Relief flooded Andrew, and he squeezed her fingers. "You do yourself credit with your concern, but you need not worry. Your gown has been paid for."

She froze, her fingers stiff in his. "How do you know this?"

"Because all my mother's bills are sent to my steward, and I just happened to see the one belonging to this scheme of our mothers. It is a gift from us to you, Mary. Do not distress yourself over the cost."

He expected relief to overtake her as it did him, but her brows only furrowed further. "But how am I to repay you? I cannot until after I wed, and I do not wish to make you wait—"

"I will not accept your money, Mary." The idea of accepting money from Lockhart made Andrew want to vomit.

She looked up sharply. "Because I am poor?"

Andrew's heart pounded furiously in his chest, her nearness, her skin on his bewitching him. Tightening his fingers around hers, he hoped to impress upon her the sincerity of his feelings.

"No, Mary. Because I love you."

Her eyes rounded further. She pulled her hands from his and backed against the wall, shaking her head. "You shouldn't say such things."

"Why not? It is true."

"I am not *free*."

"You are not yet married, either," he countered, stepping closer. "Contracts can be broken."

"And then my father will be sent to prison."

Andrew shook his head. "I will pay his debts. I care not for the cost. I will do anything to make you happy."

Surprise fell over her face. "I couldn't ask that of you."

"You are not asking it. I am offering."

Mary's eyes held his, pained. She looked as though she wanted to step forward but was resisting. Andrew yearned for her to relent, to surrender her misery and find happiness with him.

She leaned further back, widening the chasm between them. Did she not realize that all it would take to close the distance, to yield to happiness, was one step forward? "Mr. Lockhart is not the sort of man to let things go easily. He could sue. No, the cost is not worth—"

Andrew's hands came up, cupping her cheeks and effectively cutting her off. Her silky skin was smooth under his thumb as he brushed it over her cheekbone, hoping to bore into her the depth of his feelings through his eyes. He recalled seeing Lockhart with the widow, Mrs. Dobson, and his body clenched. The way Lockhart had cradled the woman close to his side, buying her perfume—those were not the actions of a man in a platonic relationship. Above all, Mary deserved to marry a man who would cherish her, and her alone.

His voice was low, and he hoped it conveyed the depth of his earnestness. "It would be worth spending every last penny I have to see you freed from the clutches of that idiotic upstart. He does not deserve you, Mary."

Her lips parted, and he was utterly enthralled by them. "But, I…"

Andrew waited, but she had no argument. He swallowed, prepared to press his advantage. "I will work every day of my life to try and be worthy of you."

Her hands came up and cupped his, but her eyes turned sad. "It wouldn't be right. I have signed a contract."

"To the devil with contracts," he whispered. "What are they when compared to love?"

"I don't...I guess..." She dropped her voice. "You truly love me?"

"Yes." He felt her resolve melting, the tightening of her hands over his own. The gentle curve of her lips in a smile was the invitation he needed, and he moved closer, his lips aiming for hers.

"No, I am still engaged," she said, halting him when he was only a breath away. He could feel her words, so close he was, and his body ached. "If I am going to kiss you, I must break things off with Mr. Lockhart first."

Andrew turned his head away, sighing, despite the hope that surged into his chest. His fingers brushed her cheeks one more time, and he looked back into her eyes. "You are bound to be the death of me. You know this, yes?"

She smiled softly, a radiant glimmer in her eyes reaching his heart. "I think I understand. But you know it is the right thing to do."

"Blasted conscience." He stepped away, his hands dropping from her face as he shook out his limbs and tried to restore his pulse to normal. When he walked back toward her, Mary was holding the box, her door open.

"I will see you downstairs in a bit?" he asked.

"Yes. You will." She smiled, and it was the loveliest thing he had ever seen.

"Good."

She disappeared within her bedchamber, and Andrew moved toward the stairs, unable to dampen his grin.

He was in love with a woman who had agreed to cancel her engagement, who agreed to let him love her. Nothing in the world could possibly ruin his happiness now.

Voices in the entryway drew his attention, and he made his way toward them, startled to come upon Finch speaking to a gentleman in a vivid violet waistcoat and starched shirt points that reached his cheekbones. Mr. Lockhart.

"The gentleman wishes to see Miss Hatcher," Finch explained, as though the situation needed any explanation.

"Of course. Allow me to see you into the library, and she will be down shortly," Andrew said, his voice clipped. He moved to go, the heavy footsteps of Lockhart's boots trailing behind him.

Well, he needed to amend his earlier thought. Nothing could ruin his happiness, but Mr. Lockhart sure knew how to put a damper on it.

CHAPTER 24

*M*ary's heart raced as she approached the library door. The organ had hardly been given the chance to calm after Lord Sanders's confession when Finch had knocked to inform her that Mr. Lockhart was awaiting her, and anxiety made her pulse race again.

It was all happening so quickly, and her heart battled trepidation with excitement. Lord Sanders's words rang in her mind, his declaration of love bolstering her confidence. He was correct; contracts *could* be broken.

She paused in the corridor, steeling herself against Mr. Lockhart's haughty arrogance. He would not take to this kindly, of that she had no doubt. But it must be done. Theirs was a business arrangement, was it not? And one made two years before. Surely there were other young women with better entries into the *ton* who could easily serve his purposes.

Mary had merely been a convenient option, her estate so near his and her father in such financial distress as to make marriage with her an easy arrangement.

She pushed open the library door. Mr. Lockhart waited near the window, his hands clasped on the top of his walking stick as he gazed outside. She closed the door behind her and crossed the room.

Mary could do this. She could be strong. She merely needed to remind herself of the look in Lord Sanders's eyes when he had professed his feelings for her, and the warmth that had enveloped her when he'd cradled her face in his strong, capable hands.

He'd nearly kissed her. And she'd nearly allowed him to.

She shoved away her regret at forcing him to wait. It wouldn't have been right. Not while she was engaged to another man. Mary cleared her throat. "Good morning, Mr. Lockhart."

He pivoted, facing her, and a brief smile flickered over his lips. "Good morning, madam." He dipped into a bow, and she crossed the room to face him near the window.

"I was hoping to speak to you today and ensure that we understand one another," he said. "I will see you at the ball tomorrow night, of course, but then I plan to leave London the following morning. I will not see you again until we are both in Berkshire some time later."

"Do you not travel directly to Berkshire, sir?"

"No. I have some business in Portsmouth which has recently been brought to my attention, and I must see to it before I return."

She nodded. None of this would be relevant to her soon. "There was something I wished to say—"

"You know that part of our agreement hinged on your ability to introduce me to men of power and prestige so I might further my name and, of course, my business. I was recently in a situation where I had hoped our connection would smooth the road for me, but alas, it came to nothing…I cannot help but wonder what you've done during my absence to fulfill your part of this arrangement."

The invitation to the Brights' summer house party. She had yet to secure an invitation. But if she was not going to marry Mr. Lockhart, then surely he would not wish for their acquaintance to last any longer. "There is something I wish to say—"

"It can wait. I came here with the express purpose of discovering in what way you plan to help me. It was part of our agreement."

She swallowed. "Which is precisely why I need to speak with you first. I wish to dissolve our agreement."

Mr. Lockhart turned to stone, his mouth neither a frown, nor a smile, and his placid expression unnerving. His silence stretched, and she took that as a reason to continue.

"We will repay the debts you paid on my father's behalf. Surely there is a woman more qualified than I to lead you into the higher circles you wish to join."

"You cannot," he said.

She'd expected this. Of course he would not take kindly to a break in the agreement, but surely they could resolve this quickly and in a way that was agreeable to both parties. "I am not certain of the specifics of what our arrangement is, but if you would only agree to sit down with—"

"No. You do not understand." His smile was easy, too comfortable, and it unsettled her. "You will not break off this engagement. You have signed the papers, your father has signed the papers, and if you walk away from me now I have the power to throw you in prison for it."

She tried to steady her hands by clutching the folds of her gown. "You will be repaid. I assure you that you will see every penny you gave my father for his debts."

Mr. Lockhart's smile widened, and he took a step toward her. He was closing in on her much like Andrew had, only this time she felt threatened. She forced herself to stay where she was.

"I did not pay any of your father's debts, Miss Hatcher. He paid them himself."

Shaking her head, she refused to believe it. She knew this man saved her family from the poorhouse and her father from debtor's prison.

"What I did," he continued, taking another step closer, "was purchase your house. With that money, your father likely took care of his own debts, but I did not pay anything on his behalf. I would never make so foolish a business decision as that."

Mary felt suspended, as though the floor had disappeared from beneath her. Father had sold this man her home? Mr. Lockhart owned the very place she lived, the place Mama was comfortable, at ease, where her anxieties did not rule her. She shook her head, unable to believe her father could do such a thing.

"Will you not sell it back to us?"

"Never." The word was spoken so carelessly, so simply, that Mary flinched. "And I will not allow you to break the contract, so put the thought from your mind. I expect you to find a way to create an entry for me into the Fashionable World, and I expect you to tell me how you plan to do so. I do not allow my workers free rein to accomplish my goals. We have a plan, and we move forward accordingly."

So he considered Mary another of his workers. A woman he could command, who served a purpose in his life. She had suspected this but hearing it from his lips was like slamming a door on the possibility of anything else.

"And if I refuse?"

"Do you have a choice?" he asked.

No. She did not. The life he painted for her was bleak, but it was what she had originally agreed to. It only appeared dimmer now because of the light Andrew had brought to her life. How he had shown her the possibility of something different. Had her hope truly soared only an hour ago?

But it did not matter. She could never displace her mother, not when it was in her power to keep their home. Mama's struggle with leaving her house was great. She could hardly manage the outing to church every Sunday, and it had taken nearly six months for Father to convince her that a trip to London for Mary's trousseau was necessary —Mary recalled well the week leading up to their departure and Mama's fits of anxiety. How could she refrain from doing everything in her power to keep their home, for her mother's sake?

With a broken heart and a resolved spirit, Mary turned to Mr. Lockhart. "Very well. I will consider how I can achieve what you ask of me, and I will—"

"No, that is not good enough. The ball tomorrow. You will make introductions there. That is a good start."

"I will do what I can, but you must know that I've hardly come to London and my list of acquaintances here is small."

He looked at her sharply. "You are staying in the home of an earl. Do not tell me you are unable to hold up your end of the deal. You will find a way to introduce me to those who might further my status or business."

Mary only nodded. He was impossible to reason with.

"Good. Then until tomorrow." He did not bow, but merely grasped his walking stick and strode from the room.

Mary was numb, the whirlwind of emotions she'd gone through that morning running through her body and over and over in her head. Despair, hope, dread, resignation. *Love.*

Oh, dear. How was she going to tell Andrew?

Wringing her hands, she paced across the room, her gaze following the tread of the oak floorboards, when boots stepped into her way and she paused, trailing her gaze up his legs and to Andrew's handsome face.

"I have been eagerly watching out the window, waiting for his departure," Andrew said, anxious eyes flitting over her.

She shook her head, and the earl's face contorted into one of concern. "What has happened?"

"It will not work."

He crossed the space, reaching for her, but she pulled back, shaking her head. "No. It will not work."

"Do not underestimate my fortune, Mary. Whatever he has asked, I can pay it."

"If that were the only problem—but it is not."

"Then what is?" he asked, pleading. "I cannot help you if you do not tell me."

She shook her head. "He has bought my house already, Andrew. He owns my father's estate."

He paused, his eyes shifting as though he was trying to sort out the problem.

"And I cannot, I *will not* sacrifice my mother's happiness for my own. She will not be happy anywhere else, and I will not submit her to losing the only place she feels comfortable. I will not do it."

Andrew said nothing, his mouth slack as he stared at her.

She needed to drive home her unwillingness to budge on this matter. "My mother has anxiety of the acutest kind, and she would not survive if she was forced from our home. Mr. Lockhart made it perfectly clear that he will not sell the house, and that he will sue if I break the contract. I have made my mind up on this matter, and I refuse to change it. Put it from your mind, Andrew, please."

"Put it from my—are you mad?" He looked up, his face stricken. "How do you propose I do that? I confessed my *love* for you, Mary. You are everything that is good, and kind, and lovely in this world, and I don't want you sacrificing yourself. I doubt your mother would wish it either."

"Of course she wouldn't wish it. If I were to tell her where we stood, she would undoubtedly advise me to do whatever I needed to be happy. But what about her? What about her happiness? If she is allowed to sacrifice on my behalf, can I not do the same for her?"

He looked stung. But what could Mary do about it?

"I beg you to reconsider."

"I will not." It was her turn to beg, for her voice to turn sad and soft. "Please, do not ask it of me. How could I be happy knowing I ruined my mother's contentment?"

"How can you be happy if you don't?"

She lifted a shoulder. "It is not meant to be."

Mary left the room, running from the man she loved before he could say or do anything to stop her. Climbing the stairs to her bedchamber, she let herself inside and locked the door behind her. Sliding onto the floor, her back resting on the door and her gown in a heap around her, Mary lowered her head into her hands and cried.

CHAPTER 25

*A*ndrew had never been one to mope. When he lost a wager—
which generally occurred half the time—he paid his debt and
moved forward. What good did it do to feel sorry for oneself? It did
nothing to change the circumstance.

But as he woke on the twelfth day of Christmas, his heart was list-
less, his motivation absent, and he realized that this despondent
feeling was likely what led most people to mope. He understood the
temptation now. He would have liked to remain in his bed all day,
reading a well-adored book and taking his meals on a tray.

If only it was not his mother's last day in London. Otherwise, he'd
allow himself to do just that.

Rising, his gaze flitted to the brown paper-wrapped package sitting
on his dressing table. He had meant to gift the book to Mary as a
surprise before she left London, but would she accept it now?

He thought it unlikely.

She had not been rude to him since the rejection yesterday, only
mildly distant. Even going so far as to refrain from holding a conversation with him at dinner. Only when Caroline had begged the group to
play her favorite game, Do Not Smile, had Mary claimed a headache

and retired early. Andrew had a feeling that he or she would have won every round had they played the game.

A knock on his door preceded his valet, and he welcomed the man to help him ready for the day.

"You've got a note, my lord," the man said, pointing to a folded sheet of foolscap on the mantel.

How had he missed that? Hope surged in his chest, quickly to die when he recognized his mother's hand.

Come see me when you have a moment, if you please. Yours, Mother

He dropped the note on his table and sat, tilting his mirror to begin his shave. He thought of breakfast the day before when Mary had made a joke about his nonexistent beard, surprising him. He hadn't expected something so silly, and she had a fun way of bringing out her playful side when he least expected it. He quite liked that about her.

He dressed quickly and went in search of his mother, pleased to find her alone in her dressing room. He wasn't quite sure what he would say to Mrs. Hatcher when next he saw her. She usually kept her distance, quietly observing their group or linking arms with his mother and chatting softly. He hadn't had much time for conversation with her before now. But he also hadn't made time for it.

"Andrew, please come in," Mother said, lowering her teacup to the table beside her chair. She smiled warmly at him, and he tried to return the gesture, but his heart wasn't in it.

"You needed to see me? Is anything the matter?"

She watched him with the precision of a mother who knew something was not quite right with her child. "The servants are already preparing our things so we might begin our journey home tomorrow with the Hatchers. I wanted to ask what the likelihood was that I could convince you to join us in Cheshire."

"Oh." He hadn't expected that.

She must have read the emotion on his face. "Is it very distasteful? I admit I do not know what value you see in London that surpasses the appeal of Brightly Court."

"Friends, entertainment, and quite a lot to busy oneself with," he said. But even as the words left his mouth, he found himself wondering where the appeal was in such empty gratification. At Brightly Court, he would miss the gaming halls and the theater, but he could ride, fish, hunt, and spend a good deal of time with his sisters. Perhaps those physical exertions were just what he needed to work through his feelings.

"I will never understand what draws you to those things. There is entertainment to be had in Cheshire as well. Though perhaps it is too stale for a young man such as yourself." Mother picked up her teacup and took a sip, seeming to weigh her words before leveling him with a look. "I have never tried to persuade you to do that which you are not comfortable with, or not ready for, especially with regard to your title."

"I have always appreciated that about you, Mother."

She lifted a hand. "Then keep that in your mind when you hear what I am about to say. My purpose is not to extricate any guilt from you, Andrew, so please understand that I mean this with love. But I wonder if you might find more satisfaction in stepping into your role a little more, in filling your father's shoes more fully."

"As the earl?"

"I realize that you do your part in parliament and care for the tenants as well as you are able. This is not a criticism. But as a mother, you must see that I only want what is best for you, and I only wish for your happiness."

He reached across the empty space between their chairs and laid a hand over hers. "I know this, Mother."

"Then will you not return home with us?" she pleaded. "Be at the estate. Manage your own affairs. You may find that it brings you satisfaction the way it did for your father."

"But that is the trouble," he said, pulling his hand away. "I could never fill Father's shoes. I could never be what the people expect from me."

Her lips parted, her eyebrows drawing together. "Son, what do you mean? You could be every bit the leader your father was."

Andrew shook his head. It was impossible.

She clicked her tongue. "I can tell you don't believe me, but what I do not understand is *why*."

"I am not the paragon of virtue he was." He dropped his gaze. "I do not put others before myself, fix roofs for tenants, and help estranged relatives get back on their feet. It does not matter what I do, I will never measure up to the example he set for me. I will be a disappointment."

"Oh, Andrew, how could you possibly imagine your father was a paragon of virtue?"

He looked up, finding an amused smile on Mother's lips.

She laughed. "Your father may have served his people and his family tirelessly, but he did grumble about it occasionally. He did not enjoy climbing on top of the Jeffersons' roof to repair the thatch that day, but his men were occupied with other things, and he knew rain was coming. He did not appreciate dinner parties or going to London to serve in parliament, and his most precious moments were those spent quietly at the fireside with his family. He was a grumpy man sometimes, but he valued his people, and he never wanted them to feel a burden."

"I did not realize he complained."

"Of course he complained. But he still did the work. It was odd for the Jefferson family to have an earl on their roof, Andrew. That would make most people uncomfortable, and he would have been better off allowing the servants to manage it. But he saw a need and filled it. That was just the way he was."

"He told me once that he enjoyed serving others because that was when he felt closest to God."

A tender smile fell over her face. "I do not think you can sum up your father better than that. But I will say that what mattered was what he *did* do. His service was no less important just because he would complain sometimes of his wet feet when he returned home— he would still glow from the success of having helped another. And your capabilities are no less than his. I have been watching you this last fortnight with your sisters and our guests, and time and again it has brought a tear to my eye because I look at you, and I am reminded of *him*. Do not ever say that you will not measure up, Andrew. You are absolutely capable of being just as good of an earl, and a man, and a father, as he was. You already are."

A father? Mary's face came to mind, and he closed his eyes, hoping that would chase away her round, green eyes and earnest expression.

"Please say you will consider it?"

Andrew stood. He needed to leave, to give himself time to think. "I will consider it."

"One last thing, before you go."

"Yes?"

"Did something occur between you and Miss Hatcher? Dinner felt different last night, but I could not quite figure out what had shifted."

Yes. "Would it be wrong of me to admit that I'm not a fan of her rich Mr. Lockhart?"

Mother's mouth pinched. "I'm not sure. Perhaps you ought to keep that opinion to yourself."

Too late. "But there were…circumstances…which led me to believe that he does not intend to value her as she ought to be valued."

"What circumstances?" Her shrewd gaze tore through him, and he realized a moment too late that he should not have said anything at all.

"We met Mr. Lockhart on the street when we were leaving Hatchard's the other day, and he was with a woman, the widow of his friend from Portsmouth, he claims."

"Claims? You do not believe that to be their connection?"

He sat back down, rubbing his temples. "That very well might be their connection, but I don't believe that is why he squired her about London while she shopped for perfume."

"Oh, dear."

"And Miss Hatcher knows. She claims to be unbothered by it."

Mother's face no longer betrayed her thoughts. "I see."

"This does not give you cause for concern?"

"If it does not do so for Miss Hatcher, then who am I to take issue with it?"

He swallowed his offense. "You are her godmother."

Mother nodded. "Yes. But she is engaged. She cannot very well break it off now, can she?"

"No, and she won't," he confessed. "Lockhart owns their estate. He bought it so Mr. Hatcher would have the funds to pay his debts."

Mother's eyebrows lifted. "Well, that is news."

"You mustn't tell—"

"Do not worry yourself, Andrew. I will not tell a soul. But it does explain..."

"Yes?"

Her gaze flicked over him. "I had wondered if you and she...well, anyone can see the way you look at one another."

Andrew's neck heated. Had he been so obvious? Standing, he moved to leave. "As you said, it is impossible."

"Perhaps you ought not give up hope yet."

"I have done my best, Mother, but I cannot foresee how anything will change. Things are out of my hands now."

She shifted, her gaze searching his face. "Trust your intuition, Andrew."

How could he? He was a gentleman, and Mary had expressly commanded him to put her from his mind. Impossible, of course, but he would do his best to respect her wishes. "Well currently, I am famished. Can I escort you downstairs for breakfast?"

"No, no. Thank you, dear, but Fanny is coming, and we are going to spend some time together in here. I am sad to part ways with her soon."

"If she is so dear to you, why have you not made an effort to see one another before now?"

Mother wore a sad smile. "Fanny has difficulty leaving her house. It is not a common issue, but it is a great pain to her and causes her a good deal of anxiety when she must travel. I have gone to visit her a few times, but then you children started to grow, and our visits became more infrequent until they just stopped."

Well, it was no wonder then that Mary refused to budge on the issue. Mrs. Hatcher's trials must be grave indeed if her daughter was willing to marry a man just to allow her to keep her home.

He moved toward the door.

"Andrew?"

He glanced back over his shoulder.

"You will still wear the green waistcoat tonight, won't you? Anne has begged me to let her wear her rose gown, and we worked so hard on that embroidery. I should like to see *some* of you match."

He smiled. "Of course, Mother. I would be honored to."

Even if it meant publicly coordinating his clothing with the woman he wished would agree to be his.

CHAPTER 26

The ballroom was lit with hundreds of candles lining the chandeliers and wall sconces, glittering and reflecting on the shiny, waxed floor. More people had shown up than Mary had expected to see at a ball in London in the middle of an icy winter, but she had yet to spy Mr. Lockhart among the guests, and for that she was grateful.

"You are such an image!" Lady Anne said, beaming. She had been all bright smiles and eager anticipation since breakfast that morning, and Mary hoped the ball was everything Lady Anne had wished for it to be thus far.

"Yes, perhaps we should not have agreed to wear matching clothing when attending a ball," Andrew said, sending Mary a tight smile. "I fear we may declare the wrong message."

She tried to smile back, but it was strained. Could he tell? He hadn't rested his gaze on her for longer than a second since yesterday. Even now, his gaze flitted around the guests as they lined up to prepare for the next dance.

Turning, Andrew offered his hand to his sister. "Anne, would you care to dance?"

"Yes, but I should like to catch my breath first. Perhaps the next set?"

He reclaimed his hand, nodding once.

"You haven't danced with Mary yet," Anne continued, "and you really ought to show off our mothers' embroidery."

Mary's heart leapt to her throat. She had not been asked to dance yet, for which she was glad. She was in no mood to pretend to feel anything other than the melancholic weariness that gripped her. But the idea of taking Andrew's hand and spinning under his direction was heady.

"Miss Hatcher, would you care to dance?"

Despite her better judgment, she nodded, slipping her silk-gloved hand within his and allowing Andrew to lead her to the floor. They stood across from one another, waiting for the remainder of the couples to line up, and Mary took advantage of the opportunity to look into Andrew's cool blue eyes without restraint.

Her open stare was reciprocated, and Mary felt locked within his gaze. The music began, the dance shortly following, and Mary stepped forward with the line of women. Her body began to relax as they moved through the motions, trusting Andrew to lead her through the familiar steps. She could not allow herself to imagine a life where Andrew was her partner always, but she knew if fate had thought to look kindly enough on her to have made that possible, they would likely have made excellent partners. He was a gentle leader, but firm when he needed to be. He watched her through the duration of their set with a discerning eye.

When the set came to a close, Mary laid her hand over Andrew's arm, afraid to speak. If she opened her mouth, she was sure to release the emotion welling up in her chest. She caught Mama's kind eye watching her from where she sat beside Lady Sanders, and Mary directed her attention quickly to Lady Anne, standing just before the mothers.

"You look absolutely radiant together," Lady Anne said, beaming. "You almost make me wish I had worn the green dress, too."

"Next time, perhaps," Andrew said, his voice stilted. "Would you like to dance now, Anne?"

"I should like that very much."

Andrew glanced briefly at Mary before taking Lady Anne's arm and leading her toward the center of the room, leaving Mary to stand alone. She could feel the gaze of her mother and Lady Sanders seated just behind her but refused to turn and make conversation. She needed to get a handle on her emotions first.

Crossing her arms over her chest, her fingers grazed the holly leaf embroidery on her sleeve, and she considered the love that had gone into decorating the gown. Flashes of Andrew's waistcoat could be seen between the crowd as he moved. Mary rather thought green was a remarkable color on him.

"You look nice this evening."

Mr. Lockhart's low voice near her ear was unwelcome and shocking, causing an unpleasant shiver to run down her body as it chased all warmth from her. She stepped back and curtsied. "Good evening, sir."

"Yes. Now, let us not waste any time." He glanced around the room with eager anticipation. He appeared just as excited about the prospect of meeting men of title and fortune as Lady Anne had been.

"I am afraid the only person I can introduce you to in this room is Lord Sanders, and you have already met him."

Mr. Lockhart froze, turning to face her, a quizzical look on his dark brow. "You mean to say you know *no one* beyond your own party this evening?"

"Not that I can see. I was honest with you, sir. I have not been given an opportunity to know many people in the Fashionable World."

His gaze flicked to the women seated behind her, and he lowered his voice. "But your mother is the granddaughter of an earl. Your godmother is a countess. You have connections."

"Yes, I do. With time and energy I could give you what you seek, Mr. Lockhart, but it will not come overnight. I can more easily introduce you to the gentility surrounding our homes in Berkshire. Mother has entertained frequently enough, and I know the Earl of Haversham well, and we have a baron who I could easily introduce you to at the assemblies in Derrey."

Her contributions to his station-rising schemes were as paltry as they sounded, and he did not seem to want to believe her. "But your father mentioned...surely when Lord Sanders returns he will be more than glad to perform introductions."

"Yes, as long as he is not promised to dance again."

"And your father mentioned a house party at Brightly Court every summer. I am certain that will do for us very nicely."

Mary froze. She had decided against obtaining an invitation. How could she attend a house party at Andrew's estate with her *husband*? No, she would not do that to him or herself. That was one sacrifice she was unwilling to make.

"We might be able to get introductions if we greet our hostess again," Mary suggested. She would be forced to act every bit the upstart she knew Mr. Lockhart to be, but she would do anything to remove the house party from his thoughts.

"Splendid idea." He took her arm. "Lead the way."

Mary weaved through the people, moving toward the space where Lady Rutledge was speaking to another woman.

The older woman's voice was low, laced with concern. "We are so grateful he has pulled through, of course. My poor sister, to be a widow...it does not bear thinking of."

"It is an absolute miracle," the younger woman agreed.

Lady Rutledge caught sight of Mary and her betrothed lurking nearby and lifted an eyebrow at them. Mary's cheeks flamed. She had broken at least three rules of etiquette in the last few minutes— leaving the safety net of her chaperones, and with a man, no less, approaching her hostess while the woman was in the middle of a private conversation, and eavesdropping on their conversation—but this was what Mr. Lockhart required of her. He would learn eventually that this would get him nowhere.

"Miss Hatcher, wasn't it?" Lady Rutledge asked.

Mary nodded. "And I believe you met my betrothed, Mr. Lockhart?

We are so grateful for your kindness in extending us both an invitation."

Lady Rutledge regally inclined her head but made no move to introduce Mary or Mr. Lockhart to her friend.

"I wondered if I might trouble you for some information," Mary said. "I had the opportunity recently to learn of your brother-in-law, Mr. Bartlett's, illness. That was over a week ago now, and I have been interested to learn how he is faring."

The woman looked pleasantly surprised. "He is well, in fact. Dr. Kent has deemed it a miraculous recovery, and my sister is absolutely thrilled. We are all quite pleased."

"I cannot imagine what a relief that must be."

"Indeed," she agreed.

The conversation moved no further, and Mary had no way to try and force it to. She dipped a curtsy. "Thank you, Lady Rutledge."

Mary began to walk away but only made it a few steps when Mr. Lockhart grabbed her upper arm and wrenched her to a stop.

He spoke through his teeth, low and near her ear. "That was all? You did not allow me a word, and it led to *nothing*."

Procuring a smile, Mary tried to pull her arm free. "You might notice that you are causing a scene, Mr. Lockhart. You would do well to release me."

He let go at once, and it took all of Mary's resolve not to rub her arm where he had squeezed it.

"Return with me. Now."

"To Lady Rutledge?" She did her best to swallow her disdain. "That would not help either of our cases, sir."

"It will if you force an introduction to the woman's friend."

Did he know absolutely nothing about polite society? About *any* society? "The introduction means nothing if the person doesn't care to know you. You must earn their regard, their respect."

Mr. Lockhart shook his head. "No. I know how these things work. Introductions are everything."

Oh, he had so much to learn.

"Is something the matter, dear?" Mama said, appearing by Mary's side.

She sucked in a surprised breath, glancing between Mama and Mr. Lockhart. How long had her mother been standing there? What had she heard? "No, Mama. We were only inquiring after Lady Rutledge's brother-in-law, Mr. Bartlett."

"Oh, the poor man. How is he?"

"He is much improved, actually. Dr. Kent is calling it a miracle."

"What a blessed relief," Mama said. She turned to Mr. Lockhart. "And you, sir? I hope you are well this evening."

"Quite."

"And your friend," Mama said, "what was her name? Mrs. Dobson, I believe. How is she this evening?"

Mr. Lockhart stilled, his gaze flicking between Mary and her mother. "Excuse me, but are you acquainted with her?"

"No. I've only heard of her through others. I was interested to find out that she traveled to London with you, sir, after returning to England on your boat. That is quite the consideration to show the wife of a friend."

His smile was tight. "I only did what any gentleman would do."

"And do you plan to leave her in London tomorrow?"

"I...am unsure. I have business which takes me to Portsmouth, and I have offered to escort her there before I return to Berkshire."

"How kind of you. How selfless."

Mary looked at her mother, then her betrothed. He nodded, accepting the praise, but his eyes were fixed on her, confusion clouding them. Mary looked to the place where Lady Sanders had been seated and found her watching them closely from across the room. The Bright siblings were still dancing, and Mary refused to search them out.

"I thought it would be prudent to inform you, Mr. Lockhart, that I no longer plan to return to my house in Berkshire. I have written to my husband, and he will begin overseeing the packing of our things and preparing us to move. The servants, you know, will complete the rest. As our landlord, I only thought it fitting that you know you are soon to have a vacancy."

"Mother," Mary hissed, her heart racing. "What are you talking about?"

"Perhaps this would be better discussed away from Society's nosy ears." Mama took Mary by the hand, leading her to the nearby door and out into the quiet corridor, Mr. Lockhart on their heels.

He looked agitated, his nostrils flaring over tight lips. "Please explain yourself, madam."

"I believe what I said was perfectly clear. We no longer have a need for the house you purchased from us, and as far as I am aware, there was never any lease agreement. We shall vacate it by the end of the month, and then you may do with the house what you wish."

Mr. Lockhart appeared as astonished as Mary felt. His mouth gaping, he sputtered. "I already may do with the house what I wish. It is my house."

Mama's face tightened. "Precisely."

Mary lowered her voice. "Mama, what is the meaning of this? How do you...I did not think you were aware of the particulars—"

Mama took Mary's hand in both of her own, peering into her face. "You must not feel forced to marry *anyone* unless you wish it."

"But the house. How will you...you will not be comfortable anywhere else. Your happiness, your very comfort...how *can* you manage, Mama?"

"I do not pretend that it will be easy, Mary. But I continue to remind myself that I once grew accustomed to our house after moving into it with your father. I can do so again somewhere else."

Mary's heart fluttered faster than an insect's wings, desperately seeking understanding in her mother's familiar face. "Yes, but where?"

"Lady Sanders has a lovely dower cottage on her property that has sat vacant for many years. She has invited us to remove there until we find something more permanent. Your father must find a way to provide for us, and I fear that will take an adjustment and quite a lot of time. He has only known his estate, and how to run it."

And how to run *them*. This was real. Mary had not imagined it. Her mother had truly sacrificed her needs for Mary.

"We have a contract," Mr. Lockhart spat, his hands splaying by his sides. "You cannot simply walk away unscathed. I will sue for breach of promise."

The Hatcher women faced their aggressor, and Mama stepped forward. "Do what you must, Mr. Lockhart, but I do believe you will have a difficult time finding a sympathetic jury after I bring my evidence to the courtroom."

"What evidence is that?" His gaze lifted, settling above Mary's head, and she felt the presence of someone approaching behind her.

"Your relations with Mrs. Dobson, of course," Mama said.

Mr. Lockhart looked sharply at Mama. "That will not hold up against the contract outlining the sale of your house in exchange for—"

"You don't have a leg to stand on here, Lockhart," Andrew's cool, deep voice said behind Mary, and a shiver ran down her neck. "You must realize that to sue for a breach of promise will splash your name through the papers, which cannot be good for your business. I suggest you leave, and all further communication may be conducted through my lawyer. I will have him contact you directly."

Andrew's presence alone made Mary's heart race, but his commanding tone was her undoing. She stood in front of him, chest heaving, as they watched Mr. Lockhart retreat down the corridor, toward the front door of Lady Rutledge's house.

When he was gone, Mary turned to her mother. "Why did you not say something sooner?"

"I had not yet decided what to say."

"But you have written to father—"

"Not yet," Mama said, smiling. "But Mr. Lockhart needn't know that. My dear friend learned some of the details of your arrangement this morning and set her servants on the job of locating some of the servants of the Clarendon, discovering what they could about Mr. Lockhart's relationship with Mrs. Dobson."

Mary had to assume the dear friend her mother spoke of was Lady Sanders. "But you said nothing before now."

"I learned of it shortly before the ball. I planned to speak to you about it later tonight so we could create a plan, but when that man grabbed your arm, I knew it was time to step in."

Mary stepped forward, throwing her arms around her mother. "You are truly willing to move out of your home?"

"Oh Mary, I can find a way to be happy anywhere as long as I am with your father. And besides, I think I will quite like living near my dear friend again." She pulled away, looking between Mary and Andrew, who stood a few steps behind her. "I believe it is safe to assume that you would prefer not to marry Mr. Lockhart."

"Quite safe," Mary said. She might not understand how her mother could love such a controlling man as her father, but she needn't. What she *did* understand was love. Turning to face Andrew, her heart warmed upon finding his handsome smile sitting languidly on his lips. "You heard everything?"

He nodded. "I heard everything."

Mary didn't hesitate. She took two steps to reach him, gripped the lapels of his coat, and pulled him down, crushing her lips against his. He seemed to freeze for only a moment before one of his hands went around her back, pulling her closer, the other sliding up to rest on her cheek.

Footsteps echoed through the corridor. Mary absently assumed her mother was beating a hasty retreat, and she pulled on Andrew's lapels as he deepened the kiss, coming up on her toes to reach him easier. Her knuckles rested against his chest and she released his coat, flattening her palm over his heart so she might feel its heavy beating.

Lowering her heels back to the floor, she looked into Andrew's sparkling eyes and saw her smile reflected within them. "I love you, Andrew Bright."

"So you mean to tell me you do not kiss all the gentlemen you find in corridors on Twelfth Night?"

"No, but I suppose I could make it a new habit."

"I have a better idea," he whispered with a playful smirk before he leaned in and pressed a kiss to her lips. "Why don't you make it a habit to kiss all the Andrews you find in corridors, always."

"*All* the Andrews?"

"Or maybe just this one." He leaned forward and kissed her again, his fingers threading through her hair as her body trembled with overwhelming love.

Mary pulled back. "Very well. I think I can make that happen."

"Good. Now, what do you say to dancing with your betrothed?"

She lifted her eyebrows. "I was unaware that I had one of those anymore."

He paused, looking at her as though he was gauging her sincerity. "You will marry me, won't you?"

She grew still, serious. "You do know that Mr. Lockhart may very well find reasonable cause to sue."

"Yes."

"And my parents now need a home."

"I believe my mother already offered them one."

"And I am quite poor."

"I have enough money for both of us."

"And...I have been absolutely spoiled these last few weeks. I have formed a very pleasant habit of burning candles late into the night so I might read."

He paused, his smile widening. "Will that be an expensive habit?"

"Oh, very expensive, I should think."

"Then we must economize and find a way to share the candle for late-night reading."

Mary grinned, her heart soaring. "I think we might find a way to manage that."

Andrew leaned down, laying another kiss on her lips before motioning to the door. "And now we shall dance."

"Yes, my love. Let's dance."

EPILOGUE

*a*ndrew swept into his bedchamber at Brightly Court, the afternoon sun streaming through the window and lighting the brown-paper wrapped package sitting on his bed. He lifted it, the familiar weight and shape of the book he'd bought for Mary resting in his hands.

"Where did this come from?" he asked his valet.

"I found it in your trunk, my lord. It must not have been unpacked when we returned from London last month."

"Hmm." Andrew slapped the book against his palm, debating. He only had a quarter of an hour before the Hatchers were set to arrive, and he did not know if he could make it to the dower house before them.

Well, it was worth trying. He would merely have to sacrifice changing out of his riding clothes to accept Mary and her parents.

Racing from the room and down the stairs, Andrew made his way to the dower house as quickly as his long legs would carry him. But he was not fast enough. He heard the sound of footsteps on gravel as he let himself into the house. He went upstairs, hoping to leave the book on Mary's pillow so she might find it later.

But when he turned the corner and came upon the very woman he was trying to surprise, all thoughts of the book left him. He had not seen her in a fortnight, and that was *much* too long to endure separation.

"Are you not supposed to kiss me every time you find me in a corridor?" he asked when she failed to move toward him.

"I suppose I am," she said, grinning as she stepped forward. Andrew slid his arms around her waist and pulled her close, breathing in her familiar floral scent and relaxing his shoulders when her lips met his.

Mary pulled away, leaning back so she might look into his eyes. "What are you holding?"

"Oh, this?" he asked, grinning. "Just a little surprise for my future wife. Would you like it now, or later?"

"Now, of course."

Andrew handed her the package and gave her enough room to open it, watching her unknot the twine and pull the paper free. After she read the title on the book, she glanced up at him. "You remembered."

Of course he remembered. The moment Caroline had mentioned that Mary had wanted to purchase *Evelina*, Andrew had stored the information away.

"I went back the following morning and purchased it for you."

"You are determined to keep me satisfied with books, are you not?" She gazed up at him with adoration. "I am not complaining. I rather like it."

"I'll keep you in full supply of books, and you'll keep me in full supply of kisses."

She grinned. "I think I can grow accustomed to this currency."

Caroline raced up the stairs, nearly knocking into them. "I've found you!" she squealed, barreling into Mary's side and forcing Andrew to move back and allow them more space.

Anne came up the stairs a moment later at a relatively normal pace, but her smile was no less bright. "Move aside, Caro. I would like a hug, too."

Caroline stepped back and Mary pulled Anne in for a hug.

"I have missed you both," Mary said.

Anne nodded. "Two weeks was far too long. Please tell me you've removed everything from that wretched house, and you are here to stay for good."

Mary glanced over Anne's head, catching Andrew's eye. "Yes, Anne. I'm here to stay. For good."

Anne clapped her hands together. "Fantastic! Then shall we return to Brightly? I have just the grandest idea for a game."

"I cannot come yet. I need to help my parents settle in."

Caroline pouted. "Leave that to the servants, Mary. You and your parents *must* come up to Brightly right away."

"Well, I suppose it would not hurt to ask them."

The sisters turned and ran down the stairs, and Andrew slipped his hand around Mary's, pulling her close to his side. "Before we reunite with my enthusiastic sisters, I wanted to let you know that I had a letter from Mr. Lockhart. He has agreed not to press you for breach of promise."

"Did you have to pay him quite a large sum?"

"No," Andrew said. "But my lawyer sent him a detailed letter explaining the very public process we would have to endure and how it might harm his business and his name in Polite Society. He was very eager to avoid any possible chance of damaging his good name."

Mary looked relieved.

"And now that I have his promise in writing, we need not fear future retribution."

"Oh, that is good news. Mama and Father will be so glad to hear it."

"And you?" Andrew asked.

"I shall be very glad if I never have to hear his name again." She paused at the top of the stairs, looking about her in the brightly lit corridor. "I think we shall like it here very much."

"The wedding is next week." Andrew took her hand in his. "You will not have to remain here long at all."

"No, but my Mama is about to make this her home, and I think it will do very nicely." She turned toward Andrew and smiled, her large, green eyes shining from the afternoon sun streaming through the windows. "I am so glad you ran into me at the Frost Fair."

AUTHOR'S NOTE

The Thames really did freeze over in February of 1814, and the people of London did hold a Frost Fair on its uneven, sturdy surface. The Belles of Christmas authors chose to move the dates of the fair to the week leading up to Christmas to better serve our stories, but the rest of the information is correct. They had printing presses on the ice which printed leaflets to be purchased as souvenirs, and sold a variety of goods such as gingerbread, roasted mutton, and Old Tom (gin). And an elephant really did walk across the ice! Due to the construction of a new London bridge with larger arches the river was unable to freeze again, and the Frost Fair we wrote about in 1814 was the final one held. I hope you enjoyed learning a little about this fascinating bit of history!

ABOUT THE AUTHOR

Kasey Stockton is a staunch lover of all things romantic. She doesn't discriminate between genres and enjoys a wide variety of happily ever afters. Drawn to the Regency period at a young age when gifted a copy of *Sense and Sensibility* by her grandmother, Kasey initially began writing Regency romances. She has since written in a variety of genres, but all of her titles fall under sweet romance. A native of northern California, she now resides in Texas with her own prince charming and their three children. When not reading, writing, or binge-watching chick flicks, she enjoys running, cutting hair, and anything chocolate.

Made in the USA
Las Vegas, NV
24 May 2021